Pokémon®
ADVENTURES

Volume 3
VIZ Kids Edition

Story by HIDENORI KUSAKA
Art by MATO

English Adaptation/Gerard Jones
Translation/Kaori Inoue
Miscellaneous Text Adaptation/Ben Costa
Touch-up & Lettering/Wayne Truman
Design/Sean D. Williams & Sam Elzway
Editor, 1st Edition/William Flanagan
Editor, VIZ Kids Edition/Annette Roman

VP, Production/Alvin Lu
VP, Publishing Licensing/Rika Inouye
VP, Sales & Product Marketing/Gonzalo Ferreyra
VP, Creative/Linda Espinosa
Publisher/Hyoe Narita

© 2009 Pokémon.
© 1995-2009 Nintendo/Creatures Inc./GAME FREAK inc.
TM & ® are trademarks of Nintendo.
POCKET MONSTER SPECIAL 3
© 1998 Hidenori KUSAKA/MATO
All rights reserved.
Original Japanese edition published in
1998 by Shogakukan Inc., Tokyo.

The stories, characters and incidents mentioned
in this publication are entirely fictional.

No portion of this book may be reproduced or transmitted
in any form or by any means without written permission
from the copyright holders.

Printed in the U.S.A.

Published by VIZ Media, LLC
P.O. Box 77064
San Francisco, CA 94107

10 9 8 7 6 5 4 3 2 1
First printing, October 2009

A mysterious Pokémon trainer—and thief!—who Red met in Celadon City.
GREEN
WARTORTLE
CHARMELEON
BLUE
Red's rival, who likes to use Charmeleon in battle. A braggart, but actually quite a skilled trainer.
MAIN
JOURNEY
As Red and Blue follow a similar path, challenging the gym leaders of each city, Red has to either compete against Blue or join forces with him to defeat those who would stand in their way. At the top of their list of enemies is the evil organization Team Rocket, a group that secretly harbors gym leaders in its ranks!
VIRIDIAN CITY GYM LEADER
GIOVANNI
SAFFRON CITY GYM LEADER
SABRINA
FUCHSIA CITY GYM LEADER
KOGA
VERMILION CITY GYM LEADER
LT.SURGE

CONTENTS

ADVENTURE 28
Peace of Mime 7

ADVENTURE 29
Go for the Golbat 21

ADVENTURE 30
Zap! Zap! Zapdos! 35

ADVENTURE 31
The Art of Articuno 49

ADVENTURE 32
A Little Kadabra'll Do It 63

ADVENTURE 33
The Winged Legends 79

ADVENTURE 34
And Mewtwo Too?! 97

ADVENTURE 35
And Mewtwo...Three! 111

ADVENTURE 36
Drat That Dratini! 125

ADVENTURE 37
Golly, Golem! 139

ADVENTURE 38
Long Live the Nidoqueen?! 155

ADVENTURE 39
Just a Spearow Carrier 169

ADVENTURE 40
A Charizard...and a Champion .. 190

28 Peace of Mine

B-BUT WHAT ABOUT THE POKÉMON THAT I GAVE TO PROFESSOR OAK...USING BILL'S TRANSPORTER?!
GASP

EEVEE IS...G-GONE !!
EEVEE
EVOLUTION POKÉMON
HEIGHT: 1' 0"
WEIGHT: 14 LBS
No. 133
One of the rarest Pokémon with an irregular genetic code. Able to evolve into any of three highly distinct, advanced forms.

ZIP
TAKKA TAKKA

...
IF YOU ASK ME, RED... YOU'RE THE REASON THEY ATTACKED THIS PLACE.

CHK
BUT THE POKÉMON THAT I SENT OVER HAVEN'T BEEN TOUCHED...

WHAT ?!

!
THAT'S WHAT YOU GET FOR TRYING TO BE EVERYONE'S PROTECTOR!

LISTEN UP, RED.
I'M GOING TO DEAL WITH TEAM ROCKET, OKAY? YOU STAY OUT OF THIS.
WAP
I REALLY DON'T CARE IF TEAM ROCKET WANTS TO BUY, SELL OR EXPERIMENT ON POKÉMON...
THEN YOU'RE THE ONE WHO BETTER STAY OUT OF IT!
WH... WH... WH...
DO YOU KNOW WHY MY GRANDFATHER BUILT HIS RESEARCH CENTER IN PALLET TOWN... OUT HERE IN THE MIDDLE OF NOWHERE?
THE DAY YOU AND I MET, MEW, THE RAREST OF ALL POKÉMON, WAS SIGHTED HERE. TAKE A GUESS WHY.
YEAH, I FIGURED THAT WOULD BE A BIT BEYOND YOUR MENTAL CAPACITY. WELL, CONSIDER THIS...
...

A "PALETTE" IS THE BLANK SURFACE AN ARTIST MIXES PAINTS ON! PALLET TOWN WAS PRISTINE... UNTIL THEY CAME!
THIS IS THE ONE PLACE ON EARTH WHERE POKÉMON AREN'T THREATENED BY POLLUTION!

WHOOSH
BLUE!!
SO YOU- STAY OUT OF THIS!

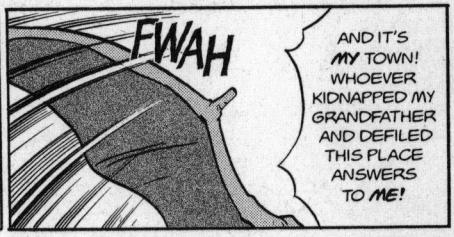
FWAH
AND IT'S MY TOWN! WHOEVER KIDNAPPED MY GRANDFATHER AND DEFILED THIS PLACE ANSWERS TO ME!

PALLET TOWN IS MY HOME-TOWN TOO!!
BOM

WHO IS HE TO TELL ME TO STAY OUT OF THIS?!

HYOOOOOO
...

FOOOOSH
SAFFRON CITY, WEST EN-TRANCE...

THE BARRIER'S SO...HUGE! IF A SINGLE POKÉMON IS PROJECTING THIS ENTIRE THING...
...I BET THERE'S A WEAK SPOT... LIKE...AT THE VERY CENTER ?!

THE STRENGTH OF THE BARRIER IS THE SAME AS BEFORE, BUT...

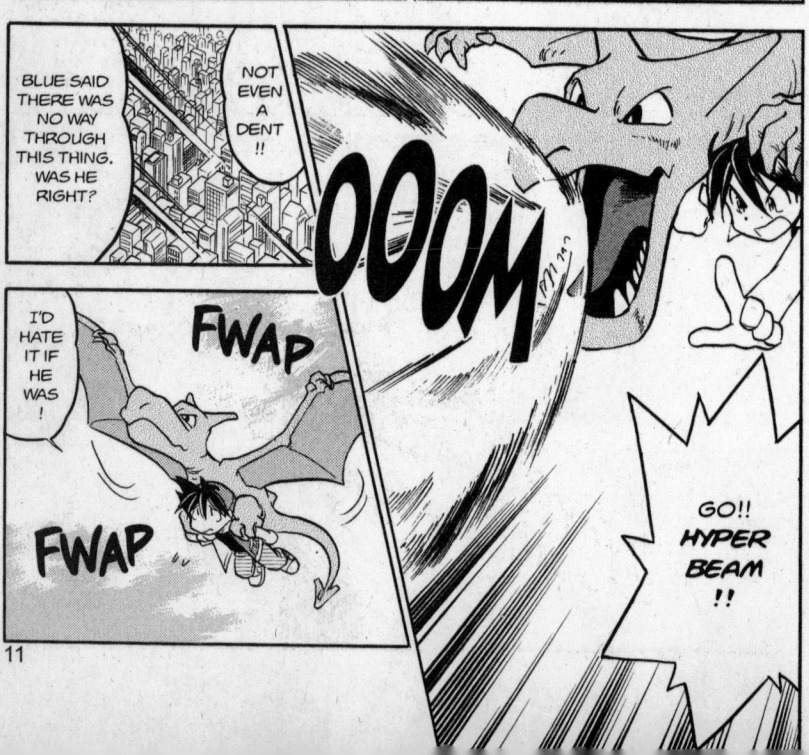
BLUE SAID THERE WAS NO WAY THROUGH THIS THING. WAS HE RIGHT?
NOT EVEN A DENT !!
OOOM
I'D HATE IT IF HE WAS !
FWAP
FWAP
GO!! HYPER BEAM !!

LET'S GO! AERO-DACTYL! UP!
WAIT...WAIT... WAIT!! SO IT'S SOLID ALL AROUND THE BOTTOM... BUT WHAT ABOUT THE TOP...?!
HMMMM
HEY! QUIT COPYING ME!
WHO'S COPYING WHO?!
!!
!
OHO... THOSE TWO!
FIGURES THEY'D KNOW EACH OTHER!

!
VMM
TOP, BOTTOM, CENTER... IT DOESN'T MAKE ANY DIFFERENCE !!
HSOOOOH
BOM
GOLDUCK!! SEARCH THE INSIDE WITH CONFUSION POWER!
BUT NOT EVERYTHING IS PHYSICAL...
TMP
SO THERE'S NO WAY TO BREAK THROUGH THIS THING PHYSICALLY...
IF I CHANNEL GOLDUCK'S THOUGHTS TO APPEAR VISUALLY IN THE POKÉDEX...
Pi Pi
SCAN IT FROM THE OUTSIDE. FIND THE LOCATION OF THE TRAINER AND THE POKÉMON PRODUCING THE BARRIER!
Pi Pi Pi Pi
GOLL

SILPH CO.
THEY'RE IN FRONT OF THE CENTRAL BUILDING. NOW AT LEAST I KNOW WHO AND WHERE THE ENEMY IS!!
SO THIS IS WHAT THEY CALL THE LIGHT SCREEN!
MR. MIME!
I'VE GOT IT! WA-HA-HA!
SHA
WHOA-HOA!
THAT STUPID BLUE FIGURED SOMETHING OUT. I KNOW HE DID! I HATE IT, I HATE IT!
PITTA PATTA
GNNNG
PIKACHU-SUBSTI-TUTE!
THIS BARRIER IS NOTHIN' TO PIKACHU'S ENERGY CLONE! TAKE THAT, BLUE BOY!
SSSLOOO

TMP
TMP
SSSLOO
PITTA PATTA
DUST
DUST BIN
VWIP
VWIP
OKAY! I KNOW WHERE THE ENEMY IS! NOW WHAT?!
OKAY! WE'RE IN! BUT WHERE'S THE ENEMY ?!
FFF
FFF
TO-GETHER YOU CAN WIN! SEPARATELY YOU CAN JUST KEEP SCORE!
WHAT DO YOU THINK THIS IS, A VIDEO GAME ?!
OH, BRIL-LIANT !!

SNORT
WE CAN'T GET YOU IN... BUT PIKACHU AND I CAN FIGHT HIM!
IT SO HAPPENS, RED...THAT I CAN TELL YOU OUR FOE'S EXACT POSITION.
NOD
NOD
GOLDUCK WILL TRANSMIT THE SENSORY WAVES IT'S READING TO PIKACHU.
GOLDUCK !
GOLL
LEAVE THE REST TO US, BLUE !!
CHK
PING

FP FP FP FP FP FP
PING
GOLLS
!
ONE FOE'S ON THE MOVE! TELL PIKACHU !
!!
VMMM
PITTA PATTA
OH!
WAAAAR
KRAKLE
KRAKLE
KRAKLE
BOING

GOLDUCK, KEEP AT IT!
M-MR. MIME IS... DISAPPEARING ?!
FP FP FP
WHAPPER WHAPPER
GOLLL
BZZZZ
BOING
NOW !!

ZAKKA
ZAKKA
ZAKKA
THUNDER-BOLT !!
FFP
WOBBLE
SHHHHHH
...
...
ZZZZ
DONK
PLOF
THEY DO ALL THE WORK... AND I GET WHAT I'M AFTER! OOOO, I'M GOOD!
KSSH
HEY! HEY!! WAIT UP!!
WOOM
WE DID IT! THE BARRIER'S GONE !!

I DIDN'T HELP YOU SO YOU COULD MAKE THIS YOUR SHOW!!
WHERE IS THE GUY I GOTTA FIGHT?! WHERE ?!
HEY! BLUE !! HOLD IT!!
SILPH COMPANY HEADQUARTERS...
I'M RIGHT HERE.

BLUE– WHERE YOU GOIN'?!
WHEN GOLDUCK FIRST FOUND MR. MIME, THIS IS WHERE THEY WERE. IT'S A CENTRAL LOCATION... WITH A MAJOR ROAD ON ALL FOUR SIDES.
VWIP
VWIP
HUF HUF
WHOA... THIS BUILDING'S PRETTY FANCY. YOU SURE THIS IS TEAM ROCKET'S HEAD-QUARTERS?
BLUE !
RED !
GAAH !!
KLONG
!
KONK
ZHP

HEH. I GIVE YOU ONE POINT FOR BREAKING THE BARRIER, BUT THAT'S ALL.
SSSSSSSSS
29 Go for the Golbat
KSHAA
SCYTHER! SLASH!
BOM
!!
PLIP
YOU'RE QUICK...
SSSSHHHH

ON YOUR SHOULDER... A GRIMER!
ZHLLLUB
GGGNNN
YOU'RE A CLEVER ONE— CHOOSING YOUR ATTACK BEFORE YOU'VE EVEN APPRAISED YOUR ENEMY. HEH...
ZZZH
YOU'RE THE ONE FROM THE POKÉMON TOWER IN LAVENDER CITY...!
TSK
SHLUBB
SHLP
N-NO...!
ZHRROOM
ZZZHHH
HURTS, DOESN'T IT?
AND WITHOUT HIS POKÉMON, A POKÉMON TRAINER IS...JUST A KID.
NN... NGH...
ZZZHH
FSHH
LAST TIME, I WAS CARELESS. THIS TIME, I WON'T LET YOU GET TO YOUR POKÉBALLS.

KRI---
WHAT... THE...?!

UNHHH...

W-WHAT'S WITH THIS WALL?!
ZAKKLE
YEOW!

WHERE AM I?! AM I BACK ON THE FIRST FLOOR?!
NO... I DON'T THINK I'VE BEEN HERE BEFORE...

VM
VM
VM
VM
YAAA!!

THESE WALLS... THEY'RE ELECTRIFIED! AND...
VWAAAAAN

...SEEMS LIKE...I'VE FELT THIS EXACT SAME SHOCK SOMEWHERE BEFORE...
TINGLE
TINGLE

BOOM
TO BE PRECISE... IT WAS ME.
TH-THAT'S IT! THE POKÉMON SMUGGLER IN VERMILION CITY! THE BAD GUY WAS A GYM LEADER...WHO USED ELECTRIC POKÉMON!!
ZAK
ZAK
ZAK
OWEEE !!
WHAT ?!
SEISMIC TOSS
YOU CERTAINLY MANAGED TO COMPLICATE THINGS FOR ME BACK THEN...
A GYM LEADER— ON TEAM ROCKET'S SIDE?!
LT. SURGE, ONE-THIRD OF THE COMMAND TRIAD OF... TEAM ROCKET!
BOOM
BYE-BYE!
KONONG
THIS TIME I WON'T GIVE YOU A BREAK!

BZZZZZZZZ
...WILL DOUBLE... EVEN TRIPLE... THE POWERS OF MY POKÉMON !
YOU MIGHT FIND THIS EVEN MORE SHOCKING... THE ELECTRICITY IN THIS ROOM...
ZAK
ZAK
ZAK
ZAK
BOOM
GYAAH !

IT'LL BE AN ELECTRIFYING BATTLE! HAHAHAAA!!

HM? A GYM LEADER? OH, YES... THERE WAS A TIME WHEN I DID SOMETHING LIKE THAT...
WHY WOULD A GYM LEADER BE ALLIES WITH TEAM ROCKET?!

B-BUT WHY-?!

IT WAS ALL A PRETENSE OF POWER!!
BUT ONLY REAL POWER LETS ME TAKE WHATEVER I WANT !!

AND WHAT DID IT GAIN ME?! WHAT ?!
I TOOK ON THE ROLE OF LEADER QUITE SERIOUSLY... WITH DIGNITY, RULES, TRAINING, "PROPER" POKÉMON BATTLES...

THE MAGNETON ON BOTH SHOULDERS PRODUCE SONIC BOOMS THAT ACT AS A DEFENSIVE BARRIER!
BLZZZZ
ELECTRODES ARE QUICK BUT LACK STRENGTH. THIS LAUNCHER HEIGHTENS THEIR POWER– AND INCREASES THEIR SPEED BESIDES!
AND IT'S ALL THANKS TO TEAM ROCKET'S TECHNOLOGY !!
CHUUU
ZAK ZAK
NOW !!
PIKACHU... READ?!
Pi
SO MUCH FOR TEAM ROCKET !!
ZAK
ZAK
ZAK
ZAK
GYAAAH!!

!!
NYAA
JUST KIDDING!
YOU'RE ON MY TURF, BOY. YOU SHOULD EXPECT THE UNEXPECTED.
...WITHOUT PUTTING ON MY INSULATED UNDER-WEAR FIRST?
KWI! KWI!
DO YOU THINK I'D ENTER AN ELECTRIC TRAP...
EVERYTHING IN THIS BUILDING IS DEVISED TO AUGMENT OUR POWER!
BY NOW, YOUR LITTLE FRIEND HAS IT EVEN WORSE, NO DOUBT...

ZAKKLE
ZAKKLE
ZAKKLE
WAGGGA !!
DSSSH
DSSSH
NOW— FIRE !!
DSSSH
ZAK
ZAK
WHY DON'T THEY RUN OUT OF POWER...?!
I...I DON'T GET IT... HE'S ATTACKING AT FULL STRENGTH... FROM THE START...
...ARE INFINITE RESERVOIRS OF POWER?! DO YOU REALLY??
NYA-HA-HA! DO YOU REALLY WANT TO KNOW?! DO YOU WANT TO KNOW WHY THEIR ATTACKS...AND MY ARMOR...
KRAKKLE
THE SOURCE OF ALL THIS POWER...
THEN TAKE THAT KNOWL-EDGE TO YOUR GRAVE!!

KRAK KRAK
KRAK
...IS THE LEGENDARY POKÉMON... ZAPDOS !!
IT...IT CAN'T BE!!
...MY POKÉMON AND I... WILL BE ETERNALLY POWERFUL!
BZZZZZZZ
Heh
THANKS TO ZAPDOS...
BZZT BZZT
WE CAPTURED IT AT THE ABANDONED POWER PLANT. AND THE LEGENDS PROVED TO BE TRUE.
KA-ZAK
WA HA HA HA !!
NOW ASK ME IF I WANT TO GO BACK TO BEING A GYM LEADER!

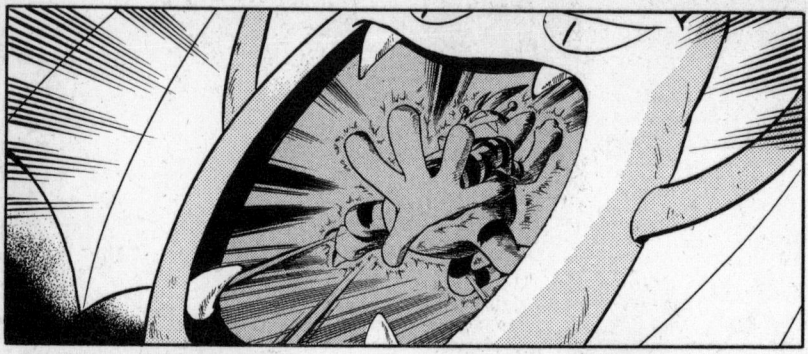

GNNG
NNGH. RED...

THERE... THAT'S WHAT'S HAPPENING ON THE FIRST FLOOR.

GN
IT'S NO USE.

NNGH

HEH... DO YOU REALLY THINK YOU HAVE THE LUXURY TO WORRY ABOUT YOUR FRIEND...?

I'LL LET YOU BREATHE... JUST ENOUGH.
GASP
KOFF KOFF
SHLP
NOW, IT WOULD BE EASY TO SIMPLY DESTROY YOU... BUT I HAVE SOMETHING TO ASK OF YOU.

NOW...HOW DO YOU THINK WE MIGHT BE ABLE TO CHANGE HIS MIND, HMMM?
...
WE'VE BEEN ASKING THE PROFESSOR FOR HIS ASSISTANCE, BUT HE DOESN'T SEEM TO WANT TO COOPERATE. TERRIBLE, ISN'T IT?
I UNDERSTAND THAT YOU'RE PROFESSOR OAK'S GRANDSON.
IT'S YOUR CHOICE. HELP US WITH DEAR OLD GRANDDAD... OR PERISH. WELL?
WAP
DO YOU SUPPOSE... IF HE SEES HIS GRANDSON SUFFER...?
NOD
...

GOING
SCYTHER !
...TO BOTH !!
N... N- NO...
IF YOU WANT TO BE SQUASHED THAT BADLY...
YOU FOOL !
WHAK
SSHHKK
RAZOR WIND!
THEN BEGONE ALREADY !

STUBBORN-NESS RUNS IN THE FAMILY.
BWAK
ZZIIUU
ZLIP
G-GRAND... PA...
HEH...
CHK
HA HA HA HA HA !!

THIS PLACE IS HUGE! TEAM ROCKET MUST BE MAKING SOME REAL LETTUCE!
TEE-HEE. AMAZING HOW FAR YOU CAN GET JUST BY SLIPPING THROUGH THE BACK DOOR!
NOW THERE'S NOTHING BETWEEN ME AND MY TARGET... 3F!!
WHAT WAS TH-THAT ?!
?
GON NNNG
!!
KRIII
OH WELL, DOESN'T MATTER... I'M HERE!!

30 Zap! Zap! Zapdos!

CAW CAW CAW

W-WAIT A MINUTE...! I THOUGHT I WAS... *INDOORS* ?!

BOM
BLASTOISE, ATTACK !!
SHAA
WELL, LA-DEE-DA!!
KCH
PFFF
HEE-HEE...
!
FSH
A MASTER OF PSYCHIC POKÉMON!!
HYPNOSIS— AND TELEPORT?!
NOW, KADABRA AND I ARE GOING TO TREAT YOU TO THE WONDERS OF 3F!!
I CREATED THE LIGHT SCREEN AROUND SAFFRON CITY. CALL ME SABRINA !
AND ONE-THIRD OF THE COMMAND TRIAD OF TEAM ROCKET.

AGH!
GNNG
MIIIIIIIIN
PSYCHIC!!
"SNORT"
PONG
PONG
PONG
MY POKÉ-BALLS...
KCH
HUH?
KCH
KCH
KDAA
KADABRA-ELIMINATE THAT BLASTOISE!
...
YOU'RE SO CLEVER... AT FOOLING SILLY BOYS.
SO IF THIS ONE FALLS... YOU'RE PRETTY WELL DONE FOR, AREN'T YOU? HEH...
SCARED AS YOU ARE, I IMAGINE YOU LED WITH YOUR STRONGEST POKÉMON.
GASHH

KRIIK
DISABLE !!
KA A A
KADABRA !!
WAK
BLASTOISE !!
THIS IS WHAT IT MEANS TO OPPOSE TEAM ROCKET!
HA HA HA! DO YOU GET IT NOW...?!
N-NO...
...WHO'S GONNA GET IT!
SHHHH
YOU'RE THE ONE...

BLAAAA
BOM!
MEGA PUNCH !!
WILL THE REAL BLASTOISE PLEASE STAND UP?!
!!
S-SO WHAT WAS THAT OTHER...?!

BOM
HORSEA !!
I CAN FOOL MORE THAN SILLY BOYS!

DWIIII
DITTO ?!

HOW DO YOU LIKE BEING BLIND?!
MWOOB
I CAN PLAY HEAD GAMES TOO, SWEETIE!

SMOKE-SCREEN !
PSHUU

VRRRRR
...THAT I CAN SEE YOU CLEARLY!
CHK
ESPECIALLY WHEN YOU KNOW...
WHERE IS SHE...?
YOU'RE TURNING ALL RED. BETTER WATCH YOUR BLOOD PRESSURE!
RRRRR
SHH
NOW, LET'S GET THIS OVER WITH!!
HEH HEH HEH...
BZZT
BZZT
BZZT
FIRST FLOOR...

ZAK ZAK ZAK ZAK
ZAK
NO MATTER HOW MUCH VOLTAGE I BLAST—ONLY YOU CAN FEEL IT!
WA HA HA HA!
GN. G
HEH
GNG
NH...
ZAKK
PIKACHU !
THUD
YAAAA !!
ZZZAKK
TRY A JOLT OF THIS !!
IVYSAUR !!
BOM
G-GOTTA... DO SOME-THING...
KCH

ZZZZZZZZAA
THUNDER SHOCK!
NO!!
ZAAA
IT'S HOPELESS! ZAPDOS!!
SHHH
SHHH
SHHH
IVYSAUR!
DOMF
AUTUMN'S COME EARLY FOR IVYSAUR THIS YEAR! WAHAHAHA!
DON'T LOSE IT...
FWSH
FWSH
IT'S HOPE-LESS, I'M TELLING YOU!
FIGHT BACK!
SHHH

HMPH. I SUPPOSE A STUBBORN BOY LIKE YOU...
...NEEDS A MORE DECISIVE BLOW.
ZAPDOS! MAXIMUM ENERGY !!
KLONG
ZZZZ
HSSIIII
THUNDER...
VZZZZZZ
GOODBYE !
ATTACK!
JUST WHAT WE'VE BEEN WAITIN' FOR! IVYSAUR!
VIIIIIII
!

SSH
SSH
SSH
SSSSSSSSS
heh
WILL IT NOW ?
NOW ALL OF ZAPDOS'S ENERGY— WILL GO STRAIGHT INTO YOUR BODY!
THE CORDS ARE CUT!
AS LONG AS I'M WEARING THIS UNDERWEAR, I CAN'T BE ELECTROCUTED !
HAHA HAHA! YOU LITTLE FOOL!
WHAT ?!
PLIP
PLIP
HM ?
PLIP

POOM
ZZZZZAAAAPP
MY SUUUUIT !!
IT'S... NOT... POSSIB...
TSSSSSS
ZZT ZZT
FUMP
IVYSAUR'S RAZOR LEAF WASN'T JUST CUTTING THE CORDS!
DIG DIG
UMMM...
JUST WHAT I WAS THINKIN', IVY!
WHEW.

VIP
...

GUESS I'LL TAKE THESE TOO...

FOUND IT! THE THUNDER BADGE !!

BZZT
BZZT
BZZT
NOTHING'S MORE POWERFUL THAN TRUE FRIENDSHIP BETWEEN A TRAINER AND HIS POKÉMON!
REMEMBER... NO MATTER HOW MANY POKÉMON YOU'VE GOT OR HOW POWERFUL THEY ARE...

C'MON. LET'S GO.

HUF HUFF
!
BAM

VWOOM

VOOM
I HOPE BLUE'S OKAY!

BLUE...!
SSSSS
LET'S END THIS!!
GOLL
GOLBAT, ATTACK!
NO!!

BOM
POLIWRATH !!
ATTACK !

EH...?
AN-OTHER VICTIM !
WRAAA

BWOOM
HYAH !!
AWWK !!

GWOOP
GYAH !!
I DO SO HATE TO BE INTER-RUPTED...
GRIM
HEH HEH HEH...
TOOM

IF YOU'RE HERE... YOU MUST HAVE DEFEATED LT. SURGE.
I BETTER NOT UNDER-ESTIMATE YOU, EH?
KKH...
31 The Art of Articuno
JINNG
AS SOON AS YOU'VE WATCHED ME DESTROY YOUR FRIEND HERE...
WELL, THEN— I WON'T.
GRIND
...HE JUST TOOK THE BRUNT OF RAZOR WIND!
YOU SEE...
NO USE.
RRG! RRG!
BLUE! WAKE UP! YOU GOTTA!

GLINT
SSHING
NOW ALL THAT'S LEFT IS... TO REMOVE HIS HEAD.
SSSS
SAY "BYE-BYE" !
!!
WAK
...
OH...
?!

GOOD JOB, PIDGEOT.
SSSSSSSSSS S

N-NO ONE... COULD TAKE A RAZOR WIND TO THE HEART...AND STILL MOVE!!
NNNGH...

MY GRANDFATHER, PROFESSOR OAK, GAVE IT TO ME!

...WEARING A PENDANT WITH REFLECTIVE POWER...?
HOW ABOUT SOME-ONE WHO'S...
CHIK

THINK YOU'RE CLEVER, EH?!

I KNEW IF I PLAYED POSSUM LONG ENOUGH, YOU'D CALL OFF YOUR GRIMER!

BLIZZARD !!
ARRRR
BOM
THEN MEET... ARTICUNO !
BACK OFF NOW—OR THIS ONE LOSES HIS HEAD!
ENJOY YOUR LITTLE VICTORIES, BOYS! THEY WON'T LAST LONG!
VSH
...
GLINT
GULP
HEH... THEN YOU'LL REMEMBER WHEN WE CAPTURED THE LEGENDARY ARTICUNO ON THE SEAFOAM ISLANDS!
YOU SAY YOUR NAME'S RED ?

W-WHAT...?!
AND IT'S ALL THANKS TO YOU!
THAT'S IT...!! HOLD IT DOWN!
FLAP FLAP
BUT TEAM ROCKET GOT WHAT IT WANTED... HEH...
IT WASN'T EASY...
WE EVEN THOUGHT WE'D LOST IT FOR A MOMENT...
AND THAT WAS THE ONLY THING THAT MADE IT POSSIBLE FOR US TO DEFEAT IT!
FWAPP
WHILE FIGHTING TO PROTECT YOU AND YOUR FRIENDS, THE ARTICUNO WAS FORCED TO EXPEND AN ENORMOUS AMOUNT OF ENERGY!
ARRR
ARTI-CUNO...
...WILL DESTROY YOU NOW!!
IN CASE YOU DON'T KNOW THE WORD, THIS IS WHAT THEY CALL IRONY! THE SAME ARTICUNO THAT SAVED YOU THEN...

HYOOOOOOO
WA HA HA HA! WE CAN MAKE ANY POKÉMON JUMP TO FULFILL OUR EVERY COMMAND!
THAT IS WHY WE THREW AWAY OUR STATUS AS INDEPENDENT GYM LEADERS! THIS IS TRUE POWER!
NOW... YOU GET IT.
RED!
PING
M-MY FEET!
THERE'S NOWHERE TO RUN TO!
RRK.
BLUE, RUN!
YOUR TURN!
TINK
NO!!
THE WALL!!
KOOM

THE SOUL BADGE?!
?!
?!
YOU BOTH SEEM TO HAVE FORGOTTEN THAT THESE TRAINER BADGES ARE MORE THAN MERE SOUVENIRS OF BATTLES!
SO YOU FINALLY NOTICED, DID YOU?
THIS ARTICUNO HAPPENS TO BE...
...UNDER THE POWER OF FOUR BADGES...
...HELD BY THE TEAM ROCKET TRIAD AND OUR EXALTED LEADER!
EACH CONTAINS A FORM OF ENERGY THAT HEIGHTENS A POKÉMON'S POWER...
...AND EMPOWERS THE BADGE HOLDER TO CONTROL ANY POKÉMON!

ICE BEAM !!
WOOSH
ARTICUNO! BLOW HIM AWAY!
UNGH !

WOO
FREEZE, BOY!

IT DOESN'T MAKE SENSE... THIS GUY'S CONTROLLING ARTICUNO TOO EASILY!
RED !
SSSS
SSS
YEEE !

HA HA HA...
WAIT! THAT'S-
THANKS TO THE POWER OF TEAM ROCKET !

SNEEEER
CHECKMATE !

FULL POWER! FREEZE THE ROOM!

TINK
TINK
...
TINK
TINK
TINK

FOOLISH BRATS!
I COULD HAVE USED YOU AS UNDERLINGS... IF YOU'D ONLY KNOWN WHEN TO ADMIT DEFEAT.
HA! TWO ICED TRAINERS, COMING UP!

HATE TO ADMIT IT, BUT THEY SURE MADE ME WORK UP A SWEAT...
SWISH!
WELL, NO NEED TO OVERDO THINGS AND FREEZE THE WHOLE ROOM...
HSSS
TONG
SSSSSSSSS
WH-WHAT...?!
N-NO... YOU WERE FROZEN!

CHARRRRR
RED !
CHARIZARD !
LET'S DO IT!

EEE-YAAA !!
ZZAK
ZZAK
ZZAK
ZZAK
TRI ATTACK !
THUNDER-SHOCK !!

I RELEASED CHARIZARD WHEN THE HOLE IN THE WALL OPENED. I FIGURED IF YOU WERE GOING TO FREEZE THE ROOM ON THE INSIDE...I'D JUST HAVE TO ROAST IT FROM THE OUTSIDE!
DOMP
YOU JUST WEREN'T THINKING ON A GRAND ENOUGH SCALE.
JANG
THE SOUL BADGE...

SSSS
PFF
PFF
PFF
YOU DIDN'T HAVE TO FLAME THE WHOLE BUILDING! THAT WAS HOT!

HEY, BLUE!

TWRL
OHH..
H-HEY...!

CAN'T TAKE IT, HM?
HEH

I'M T-TRYING TO SEE IF THE MONITOR WILL SHOW WHAT GOLDUCK IS PICKING UP MENTALLY...
...BUT SOME STRANGE PSYCHIC PULSE SEEMS TO BE B-BLOCKING IT...
BZZZZ
IT'S NO USE.

?!
GOLDUCK!
BOM

OKAY, GOLBAT... SHOW ME! WHERE IS PROFESSOR OAK BEING HELD?!
GOLL

GUESS I'LL HAVE TO FIND GRANDFATHER WITH THIS!
VIP

!
EEEEEK !!
BATT
THAT LOOKS LIKE THE BASE-MENT!
GR-GRAND-PA...!
REMEMBER WHAT KOGA SAID! USE IT!
PWAK
RED-TAKE THIS!
THAT SOUNDED LIKE A GIRL...! GREEN ?!
I'LL MEET UP WITH YOU AS SOON AS I CAN.
VOOM

32 A Little Kadabra'll Do It

HWOOO
A SMOKE SCREEN LIKE THIS IS NOTHING TO ME!
UNDERSTAND ?
WHAT I CANNOT SEE WITH MY EYES, I SEE WITH MY MIND'S EYE.
BWOOOOOO
HAI-YAA !!
HWOOOO
PSYCHIC !
GYAAAH !!
GEEESH
N-NO !
WHAT ?!
DISABLE !
KWNNNG
HHHSSSSHHH
KAW KAW
HORSEA'S SMOKE-SCREEN!

PTT
UH...
YOURS WILL BE A SHORT CAREER...
WELCOME TO THE BIG LEAGUES, DEAREST.
HEH HEH
GRNNG
NNGH... I...I CAN'T MOVE !
HA HA HA!
NNGH
BUT THEN... I GUESS FIGHTING'S ALL YOU CARE ABOUT...
Y-YOU'RE A GOOD FIGHTER, ALL RIGHT...
OH...
RRRING
YOU AREN'T CUTE 'N' STYLISH LIKE ME!
TA-DAAH
JUDGING BY YOUR FLY AWAY HAIR AND TACKY OUTFIT...
EEEEK !!
KADABRA!! ATTACK!
SLASH
JABB
CHEAP SHOTS, EH...?

GOTCHA !

BOM
CLEFAIRY! JIGGLY-PUFF!

LOST MY FOCUS WHEN SHE DISSED ME!

THIS HIDEOUS SOUND WAVE... PREVENTS ME FROM LOCATING HER...!!
AAAA-RRH !!
CLEFAIRY, GROWL! JIGGLYPUFF, SING!
I HAVE TO GET FREE OF THIS HALLUCI-NATION...

VMMM
NOW...!
POOF
AND THE HALLUCINATION GOES... POOF!
CHK
WAIT A MINUTE...!
ALL I CAN DO IS ESCAPE!
I DON'T STAND A CHANCE AGAINST HER PSYCHIC POWERS... AND MY POKÉMON ARE TOTALLY OUTCLASSED!
PWIP
IT'S MINE NOW!
SSSS
!
LONG AS I'M HERE...!
SHM
BYE-BYE-EEE! ♡

SUDDENLY I'M A LOT FARTHER UP THAN I THOUGHT... BUT STILL NO SIGN OF GREEN... HUH?!
TMP TMP TMP
YEESH... IS THIS PLACE A MAZE OR SOMETHING ?!

WHERE AM I?!

OY-SHOH
PRETTY HEAVY, THAT'S FOR SURE...

AND WHAT'S THIS?!

WE'VE GOT TO FIND THOSE BRATS FAST! BUT WE CAN'T STRAY FROM THE ROOM WITH THE POKÉMON BADGE ENERGY AMPLIFIER...
THEY'VE NOT ONLY DEFEATED SURGE, BUT KOGA TOO! AND AS IF THAT ISN'T BAD ENOUGH, THEY'VE SET THE BUILDING ON FIRE!

NO.
FIND THEM ?
GASP

KLIK
NO, MA'AM!
DID AN UGLY GIRL JUST RUN BY?
THIS THING... MUST BE IT!
POKÉMON BADGE ENERGY AMPLIFIER...?!
WHAT ARE YOU TWO DOING?!
YES, SABRINA!
YOU'RE RELIEVED OF DUTY! GO BELOW!
!
IF YOU WANT TO SAVE PROFESSOR OAK AND THE CITIZENS OF PALLET TOWN... COME TO SAFFRON CITY.
THAT'S THE ONE WHO ATTACKED THE RESEARCH CENTER!
H-HEY... THAT'S...

IS SHE LOOKING FOR THIS...?!
GLANCE GLANCE
AND SHE'S COMING IN!
KLIK KLIK

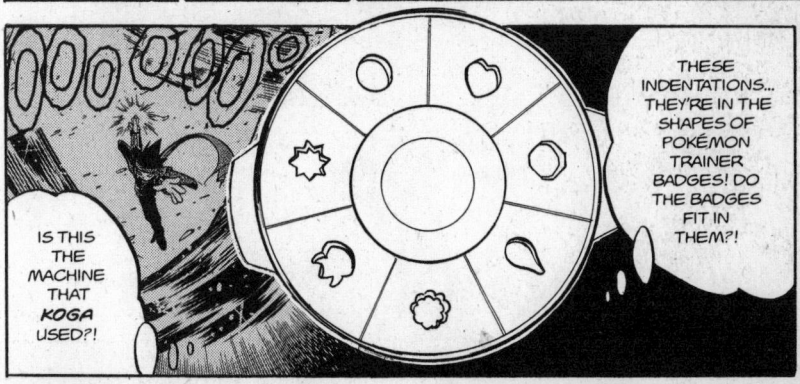
IS THIS THE MACHINE THAT KOGA USED?!
THESE INDENTATIONS... THEY'RE IN THE SHAPES OF POKÉMON TRAINER BADGES! DO THE BADGES FIT IN THEM?!

SHIP!
RSTL
...
I'VE GOT SIX OF THE BADGES WITH ME !!

WHO'S THERE...?!
EEP!!
KLONG
I ONLY NEED ONE MORE BADGE TO FILL ALL SEVEN SLOTS!!
FWAAH
VOOOON
WELL... THE BEST DEFENSE IS A GOOD OFFENSE... IN OTHER WORDS— PIKACHU!
SHH
OHO! YOU FOUND THE DEVICE, I SEE!
HOW CUTE! PIKACHU KNOWS I'M NOT REALLY AN ENEMY!
TUP
PIKACHU... WHAT'S WRONG?!
BLOOB
WAAA?!
SOMETHIN' WRONG, RED?

OOH! YOU FINALLY FIGURED IT OUT!!
BOOF
WRRRRRR
R-RIGHT...
GR-GREEN?!
NYOOP
FWOP
OH, COME ON!
SURELY YOU REMEMBER THAT I'M A MASTER OF DISGUISE!
AT LEAST PIKACHU KNEW IT WAS ME! ♡
PLINK
BASE-MENT LEVEL ONE...
THAT'S WHAT THE DISPLAY SAID, BUT...
!!
SHFF

B-B... BLUE ?!!
ARE YOU HURT?

GRANDPA !!

F...FORGET ABOUT ME. YOU'VE GOT TO... HELP THE PEOPLE OF THE TOWN FIRST. BELOW US...IN BASEMENT LEVEL TWO...
THERE'S A HUGE POKÉMON TRAINING GROUND.
ALL THE PEOPLE WHO WERE TAKEN FROM THE TOWN... ARE THERE !!

THEY WERE... TRYING TO...USE THAT P-POWER TO...
STAGGER
GRAND-PA... ?!

THE PEOPLE OF PALLET TOWN... HAVE AN INNATE EMPATHY...FOR THE FEELINGS OF POKÉMON.

...A SCIENTIST WHO ESCAPED FROM THEM.
A SCIENTIST WHO WAS WORKING...
WOBBLE
...ON... ON A TER-RIBLE... EXPER-IMENT...

NNH... I'M HURT... WORSE THAN I THOUGHT. THEY... WANTED ME TO REPLACE...

HEY, RED! TAKE A GANDER AT THIS!!
ACK!
THE MARSH BADGE! I JUST STOLE IT OFF THAT PSYCHIC GIRL! TEE-HEE!!
G-GIMME THAT, GREEN!
GIVE IT TO YOU? FOR FREE? OH, PLEASE! YOU KNOW ME BETTER THAN THAT!
BUT I'LL DO A TRADE... BECAUSE I'M SUCH A SWEETHEART! I'LL GIVE YOU THIS BADGE...FOR YOUR MOON STONE!
WHAT?!
THE MOON STONE! DON'T PRETEND YOU DON'T HAVE IT!
UHH...
I'VE GOT TO HAVE THAT STONE... IN CASE I EVER MEET UP WITH SABRINA AGAIN!
COME ON, GREEN! WE DON'T HAVE TO HAGGLE. IF WE JOIN FORCES AND FIGHT TOGETHER...
WISE UP, RED.
WE CAME HERE FOR DIFFERENT REASONS. BUT THIS TRADE WILL HELP BOTH OF US GET WHAT WE WANT.
JUST TRUST ME AND DO AS I SAY.

WHY NOT ?!

hmph
DID YOU JUST SAY... TRUST YOU ?

SIGH! EVERYTHING'S GOING EXACTLY ACCORDING TO PLAN!
GUESS I CAN'T COM-PLAIN...

THERE WE GO! TRADE COM-PLETED!
SHOOP

THANKS FOR THE INFO!
THAT DEVICE IS THEIR SECRET WEAPON. WHEN ALL SEVEN BADGES ARE INSERTED, IT GENERATES AN ENERGY THAT AMPLIFIES A POKÉMON'S POWER BIG-TIME!

HEY, RED... TO BE FAIR, I SHOULD TELL YOU...
?
HEH

ALL THE MORE REASON TO ELIMINATE YOU...AS IF I NEEDED MORE OF A REASON!!
!!

AND THE ONLY REASON I COLLECTED ALL THESE BADGES AND SNEAKED INTO THIS BUILDING WAS TO GET MY HANDS ON THAT NEW POKÉMON!
WE-E-ELL, ACTUALLY... THE REAL TRUTH IS THAT IT CREATES A NEW POKÉMON!
PLOK PLOK

THE... UH... REAL SABRINA ?
HAND OVER THAT DEVICE !
BAD ENOUGH THAT YOU MADE A FOOL OF ME...
YOU LITTLE BRATS !!
PLOK
HERE GOES NUMBER SEVEN... AND...
YOU WANT THIS, HUH? WELL, I'LL GIVE IT TO YOU!
STAY BACK !
O-KAY. ♡
ZZIP
GREEN, THIS IS DANGER-OUS!
SHHHHH
?!
AWRIGHT! HERE WE GO, PIKACHU!
ZOOM
KRAK
PSY-BEAM !!
AGH !!
IF YOU WON'T ATTACK... I WILL!
RGH...
HAND IT OVER !
GREEN... WHAT'S G-GOING ON?!

TINK!
HUH?
CHING
...
THANKS FOR EVERYTHING... SWEETIE-PIE!
GLINT
?
SSSSSSS
SORRY, RED. ♡
WHAT? YOU THOUGHT THE BADGES I "RETURNED" TO YOU WAY BACK WHEN WERE REAL?! LIKE I SAID... YOU SHOULD KNOW ME BETTER THAN THAT! TEE-HEE!
WHA... WHA...
HMPH... IN-FIGHTING! WHAT AMATEURS!
WHY... YOU... LITTLE...!
HEY!
VROOM
GR-GREEN!
I'LL LEAVE THE REST TO YOU!
BOM
COME FORTH... MOLTRES!
...
GRRN
HA HA HA...
FSH
KADABRA! BRING FORTH ARTICUNO AND ZAPDOS!
FSH

PLOK
NOW ALL SEVEN ARE TOGETHER!
POIK POIK
OKAY THEN... GET RID OF THESE FAKES... AND...
VIP VIP
THIS SHOULD BE FAR ENOUGH... NOBODY'LL CATCH UP TO ME NOW.
VOOOIN
N-NO!! IT'S FLYING AWAY!!
WHAT ?!
POOF
AT LAST... THE NEW POKÉMON IS M...
VWOOO
IT'S WORKING !!
!!
GLEEEEM
FINALLY! IT'S HERE!!
WH... WHAT THE... ?!

OOOWEEEOOOWEEE
THE FIRE'S SPREADING FROM THE MAIN BUILDING! WE HAVE TO GET OUT OF HERE!
YOU'VE GOT TO BE KIDDING ME! THOSE ARE KIDS! JUST KIDS!
!
MY APOLOGIES. BUT YOU'RE NOT GOING ANYWHERE.
RRUMBLE
RUMBLE
!!
NIXXX
ONIX! TACKLE !!
YOU FOUGHT ME AND THIS ONIX ONCE, RED...
NOW IT'S TIME FOR US TO FIGHT TO-GETHER!
SSSHHHHHH

THIS IS MISTY. I'VE GOT THE NORTHERN GATE.

ONNNNN
CHK
BROCK HERE. THE SOUTHERN GATE IS SEALED.

SAFFRON CITY IS SURROUNDED! AND OUR ALLIES, RED AND BLUE, MUST HAVE PENETRATED SILPH COMPANY'S CENTRAL HEADQUARTERS BY NOW.

ERIKA. WESTERN GATE SECURED TOO.
MY TOWNSFOLK FROM CELADON CITY HAVE SURROUNDED THE EASTERN GATE.
OOOW-EEE

GOOD LUCK, RED...
OOWEEE
OOWEEE

OUR *UNKNOWING* ALLIES, I SHOULD SAY. WE KEPT THIS PLAN SECRET FROM THEM, TO MAKE SURE THAT TEAM ROCKET WOULDN'T DISCOVER IT!

33 The Winged Legends
SSSSHHHHHHHHHH
THANKS TO THE POWER AURA GENERATED BY THIS DEVICE, THESE THREE BIRD POKÉMON HAVE PRODUCED A SINGLE LEGENDARY POKÉMON!
WHAT'S THAT ?!
GREEN...!
UNHH
AAAAGH!!
VMMMM

BLIZZARD !!
THUNDER !!
FIRE SPIN !
GAGH !
WOOM
THIS IS TEAM ROCKET'S GREATEST SCIENTIFIC ACHIEVEMENT—
KRUMPLE
THE WALL...
YES! WE EXPERIMENTED ON YOUR PRECIOUS EEVEE TOWARD THE SAME END—THE LEGENDARY PROTOTYPE, YOU MIGHT SAY!
SHAMM
EE-VEE !!
A SIMULTANEOUS STRIKE WITH THE POWER OF THREE POKÉMON AT ONCE!
THAT'S THE FATE OF ALL LAB CREATURES.
YOU CREEPS !!
AFTER YOU TRANSPORTED THE LITTLE THING TO THE RESEARCH CENTER, WE TOOK IT BACK FOR A FEW FINAL EXPERIMENTS... BUT NOW, WE HAVE NO USE FOR EEVEE ANYMORE!

WAAM
HAVEN'T YOU LEARNED YET?!
SAURRRR-R
BOM
YOU CAN'T STOP ME...
OHHH, HOW I'VE LONGED FOR THIS POWER!
IT'S NO USE !!
FYOOO
NO...
WE'VE LONG KNOWN THAT WE NEEDED ALL THE BADGES TO COMBINE POKÉMON POWERS.
VOLCANO! BOULDER! MARSH! THUNDER! RAINBOW! CASCADE! SOUL! THE POWERS OF ALL THE GYM LEADERS!
WE COULD HAVE DESTROYED YOU BOTH EASILY ANY TIME WE WANTED TO... BUT YOU STILL HAD A JOB TO DO FOR US!
SO WE DECIDED TO WAIT FOR YOU AND YOUR FRIEND BLUE TO COLLECT THEM FOR US.
SEVERAL TIMES WE TRIED FORCE... TO NO AVAIL.
NOTICE OUR CENTER WAS DAMAGED YESTERDAY BY UNKNOWN VANDALS. WE WILL REOPEN WHEN OUR MACHINES ARE RUNNING AGAIN.
THE POKÉMON CENTER
BUT TAKING THE BADGES FROM EXPERIENCED GYM LEADERS WAS NO EASY TASK!
RRRGHHH
NO WAY...

AT LAST THIS PLACE WILL SERVE A USEFUL PURPOSE!
WE'RE TAKING OVER YOUR BELOVED PALLET TOWN! WE'LL MAKE GOOD USE OF ITS UNSPOILED LAND...AND ITS PEOPLE, WITH THEIR STRANGE EMPATHY FOR POKÉMON!
...GOODBYE!
NOW I'D LIKE TO THANK YOU FOR YOUR COOPERATION AND TELL YOU...
HWOOO
GWAAHHH
GH... AH...
BZZZT
BZZZAK
THIS TOWN...
PALLET TOWN WAS PRISTINE... UNTIL THEY CAME!
THIS IS THE ONE PLACE ON EARTH WHERE POKÉMON AREN'T THREATENED BY POLLUTION!
...IS OURS!! AND WE'RE NOT LETTIN' YOU MESS IT UP!!
FWA

BLUE...!
I'VE RESCUED MY GRANDFATHER AND THE TOWNSPEOPLE! ALL THAT'S LEFT IS TO DEFEAT THIS FREAK!
ZZZH
THAT'S TELLING HER, RED!
WE'RE GOING DOWN FIGHTING!
GNAAA!
WHO YOU CALLING A FREAK? WHAT... IMPERTINENCE!!
SSS
PERHAPS EVEN AS CHARISMATIC AS GIOVANNI...? WELL...
I'M SURE YOU WOULD HAVE GROWN UP TO BE VERY HANDSOME MEN.
DOM
YOU'RE CHARMING BOYS, RED AND BLUE...
HWOOO
GUST!!
I GUESS WE'LL NEVER KNOW!

HWOOOOM
HAAA-HAHA HA!
HWOOOORRR
OH, I CAN'T WAIT TO TELL GIOVANNI ALL ABOUT THIS!
THINK! THINK!
WE'RE NEVER GONNA WIN LIKE THIS! GOTTA FIND A WAY TO ESCAPE... QUICK!
I'LL TAKE A CHANCE!
OKAY!
GNNN
GREEN REALLY WANTED THIS MOON STONE. SHE MUST HAVE BEEN PLANNING TO USE IT FOR SOMETHING!
ROLL
!
THE MOON...

SSSSSSSS
BLUE'S STILL BEARING THE BRUNT OF THE ATTACK...
NOW'S MY CHANCE...!
IF I CAN FIND A WAY TO USE THIS... ON GREEN'S POKÉMON... MAYBE...
GLEEEEM
GULP!
FWIP
FWIP
FWIP
FWIP
CLEFABLE!
PAWA WAWA WAWA
NOW!!
Q-QUICK ATTACK...?!
WHAT?!
SHOOOOM

SCRATCH
POKA
POKA
POKA
POKA
FURY ATTACK !
COMET PUNCH !
SCRATCH
SCRATCH
HYPER BEAM !
KRAK
WE'VE GOT AN ESCAPE ROUTE NOW. NEXT...
AND NOW THAT CLEFAIRY'S EVOLVED INTO CLEFABLE... IT'S SUPER POWERFUL !
METRONOME IS A SPECIAL ATTACK THAT RELEASES OTHER ATTACKS AT RANDOM!
OHHH, NO YOU DON'T!
SKY ATTACK !!

CA-BOOM
EEEE-YOWWW!
AYOOOO!
HUH? DO I FEEL... A CHILL?
NOT EVEN THEY CAN SURVIVE A FALL LIKE THAT.

SKY ATTACK AGAIN!
SSSS
TH-THAT WEB... IVYSAUR'S VINE?!
HWOOOO
INCOMING !!
GET THEM !!
WE'VE GOT SOME ATTACKS UP OUR SLEEVE TOO... THREE OF 'EM, SPECIFICALLY !
WHO ELSE ?
GREEN !
ZZZZ
BOM

VINE WHIP (GRASS)! FLAME-THROWER (FIRE)!! HYDRO PUMP (WATER)!!!
ZAPDOS! MOLTRES! ARTICUNO! ATTACK!!
HWOOOM
BOK
GRAAAAW
ATTAAAACK!!

OOMM

GWOOO
THE BUILDING'S GONNA COLLAPSE... HURRY !!
KRAK

WHAT... ?!
SHOOM
DIMM
GIOVANNI... !
YES !
...
THEY'RE... FREE !
MOLTRES ! ZAPDOS !
VWISH
VWISH
VWISH

YEAH! ARTICUNO TOO!
FWAP
KROOOSH
MOVE IT, RED!
THE BUILDING'S COMING DOWN!
...?
VIP
SNEER
WITH PROPER TRAINING, THEY'LL ALL BECOME WONDERFUL POKÉMON.
WE'VE RETRIEVED ALL THE POKÉMON THEY WERE USING.
NO ONE SLIPPED THROUGH OUR BARRICADE.
THE THREE LEADERS AND THEIR BOSS ARE ALL BENEATH THAT COLLAPSED BUILDING.
THANK GOOD-NESS EVERY-ONE IS SAFE AND SOUND.
MURMUR
MURMUR

I NEVER DREAMED TEAM ROCKET'S NEW POKÉMON WOULD BE SUCH A BEAST! SHEESH...
VIP
VIP
?
YADA YADA
...
HUH?! WHERE'S GREEN?!
WHAT'S HE DOING HERE ?!
SO MUCH FOR MY BIG PLANS...
BLUE... ?
!
VWIP
RED... I'M LOOKING FORWARD TO MEETING YOU AT THE INDIGO PLATEAU.

34 And Mewtwo Too?!

IT...
IT...
...WAS JUST A DREAM!
WHINNY
POP
UNGH!
...SO CLOSE...!
JABB
TWITCH
WOW...
ZZZMM
...
CERULEAN CITY... NORTHWEST SECTOR!!
THE BEAST OF CERULEAN CITY...?!
POKÉMON CENTER

AIN'T SURE O' NOTHIN'! WHATEVER IT WAS DEEP-FRIED THE TOWN, SLIPPED INTO THE CERULEAN CAVES...AN' IT'S MOST LIKELY HIDIN' THERE NOW!
ARE YOU SURE IT'S A POKÉMON...?!
BEAST IS RIGHT!! AIN'T NOTHIN' BUT DEVASTATION OUT YONDER! TH' NORTHWEST SECTOR'S JUST THE NORTHWEST BARBECUE NOW!
HEY, RED! JUS' 'CAUSE YOU BEAT DOWN TEAM ROCKET, DON'T GO GETTIN' UPPITY AND TRYIN' TO KETCH THAT THING, Y'HEAR?
...I'M ALREADY HERE.
HE HE HE
TOO LATE, BILL...
CHAK
POK
CE
A WHITE BODY, POINTY EARS, PURPLE EYES... WHAT IS IT?!
BUT I DIDN'T EXPECT THIS...! IT'S LIKE THE WHOLE PLACE WAS TRAMPLED BY SOME KIND OF...WELL... BEAST!
FWAP FWAP
TNN TNN
SHEEEE... WHEN I HEARD "BEAST," I FIGURED IT MUST BE SOME POWERFUL POKÉMON...

THAT'S FUNNY... THIS AREA DOESN'T LOOK BURNED OR CRUSHED...
MORE LIKE... IT WAS... TWISTED SOME-HOW.

HUH ?!

SO THIS IS THE CAVE BILL WAS TALKING ABOUT !!
SHUU SHUU

WHAT?! WHAT'S WRONG WITH ALL OF YOU?!

?

HWOOOO
UH-OH!

HOOOO

WAAAAAH!
AAAAAH!
NO... SOMETHING WEIRD IS GOING ON!
A TORNADO-?!
IT'S... IT'S COMING FROM THAT CAVE?!
HWOOOOOO
GNNG
FTCH!
EEEEEP!
AERODACTYL! HELP!! EVERYBODY!! GYARADOS!!!

GOTTA GET EVERYBODY EXCEPT AERODACTYL INTO THEIR POKÉBALLS...
HUH?! THEY'RE GONE?! WERE THEY... BLOWN AWAY ?!
FWOP
FWOP
FWOP
FWOP
AGH! IF THIS KEEPS ON, WE'RE GONNA GET SUCKED INTO THAT TWISTER AGAIN!
C-COME ON !!
HWRRRR
OHHH... SHOOT !
HWOOOOO
SLIP
OH... NO...

SNAG
HWOOOO
THIS IS NO TIME TO PANIC!!
!!
HALP !!
VNNN
RRR-AAAA !!
QUICK!! EMPTY POKÉ BALLS!!
Y-YES!! WHEW!
GNNG
POM
POM
POM
POM

BLAINE !
WELL, WELL, WELL... LOOKS LIKE IT WAS MY TURN TO SAVE YOU, RED.

THAT'S RIGHT, RED.
THIS TWISTER... IS IT COMING FROM THE "MONSTER OF CERULEAN CITY"?
HWOOOO OOOOOOO

SHHHH
BUT I'VE GOT TO DEFEAT THE THING THAT'S FORMING IT! THERE'S NO OTHER WAY!

YOU CAN LEAVE IF YOU LIKE...
UM... IT'S COMING BACK... SHOULDN'T WE, UH...?

FIRE SPIN !!
ROARRK
THIS IS NO ORDINARY TORNADO !!

AGH !!
HOOOOOO
HOOO
IT'S...IT'S BOUNCING BACK!!
ACK !!
THAT CYCLONIC ENERGY IS POWERFUL ENOUGH TO TWIST ANYTHING! IT SERVES AS AN IMPENETRABLE SHIELD BY FLINGING BACK ANY KIND OF ATTACK LIKE A BOOMERANG! THE ULTIMATE DEFENSE AND OFFENSE IN ONE, IT'S THE DREADED...
ATTACK
REFLECTION
...PSY-WAVE !!
ANY ENERGY DIRECTED INWARD IS REFLECTED OUTWARD BY THE ROTATION OF THE TORNADO. THIS IS THE MANIFESTATION OF AN EXTRAORDINARY PSYCHIC POWER.
DID YOU SEE THAT, RED ?
GASP
Y-YOU MEAN...
HWOOOORRR
THERE'S ONLY ONE CREATURE IN THE WORLD WITH THIS KIND OF POWER...!
THE MASTER OF THE PSYWAVE LURKS AT THE BOTTOM OF THE TWISTER-LIKE AN ANT LION.

HWOOOOOOOO
MEWTWO !!
YAAAH !!
HOOOO
HWRRRR
FLASH
PFFF
HEY!! IT'S D-DISAPPEARING !!
IT CONCEALS ITSELF, DEFENDS ITSELF, AND STRIKES BACK ALL AT THE SAME TIME...
AND THIS IS ONLY ONE OF ITS ATTACKS!

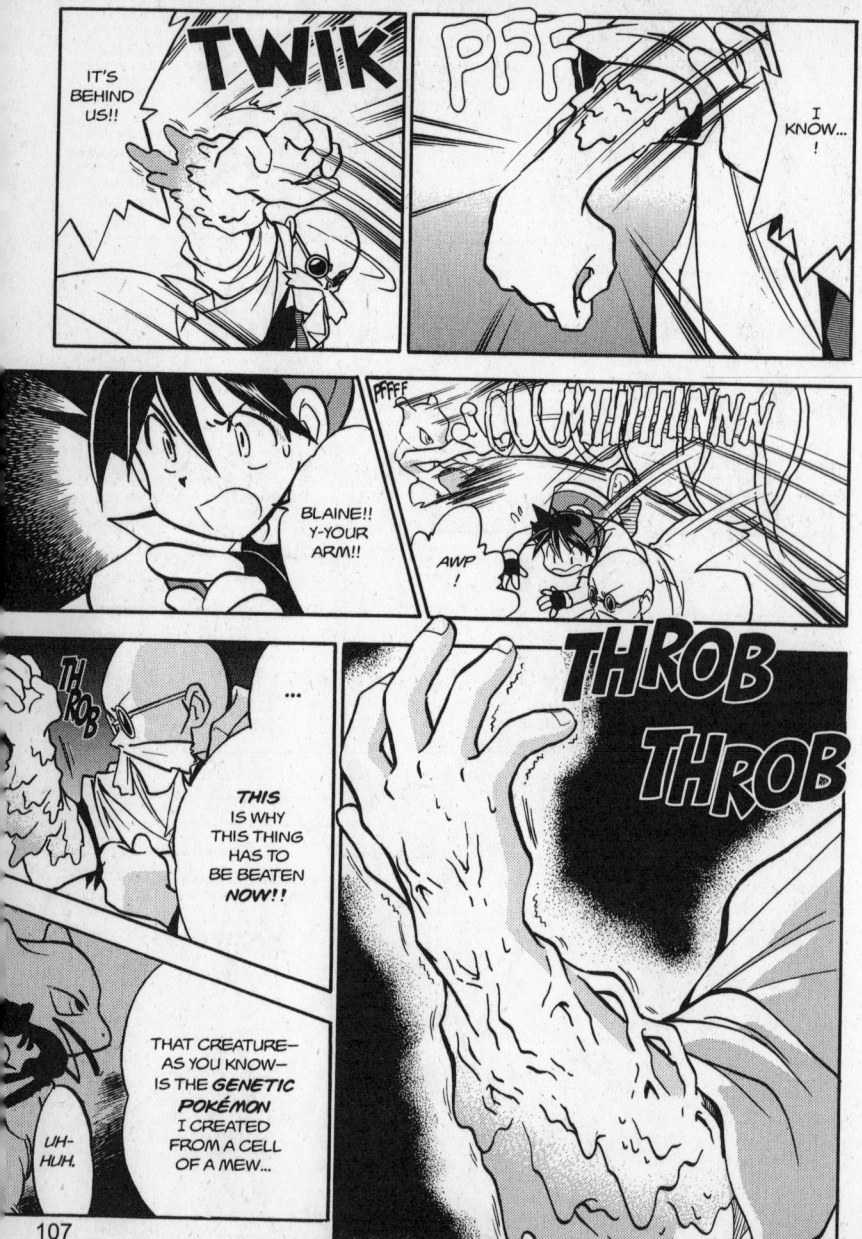
TWIK
IT'S BEHIND US!!
PFF
I KNOW...!
BLAINE!! Y-YOUR ARM!!
PFFFF
MIIIIIINNN
AWP!
TH ROB
...
THIS IS WHY THIS THING HAS TO BE BEATEN NOW!!
THROB THROB
THAT CREATURE— AS YOU KNOW— IS THE GENETIC POKÉMON I CREATED FROM A CELL OF A MEW...
UH-HUH.

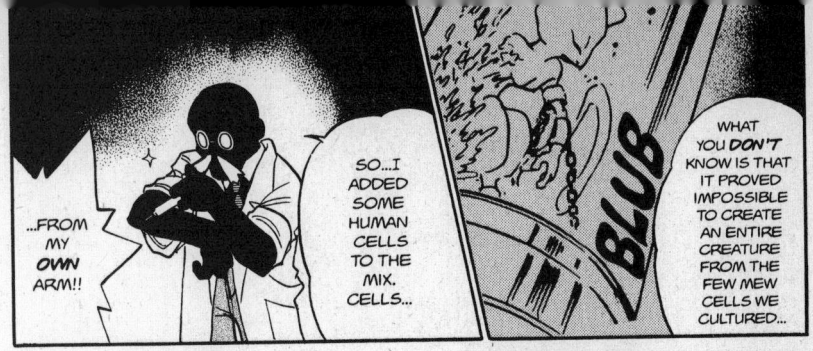
...FROM MY OWN ARM!!
SO...I ADDED SOME HUMAN CELLS TO THE MIX. CELLS...
BLUB
WHAT YOU DON'T KNOW IS THAT IT PROVED IMPOSSIBLE TO CREATE AN ENTIRE CREATURE FROM THE FEW MEW CELLS WE CULTURED...

NO! YOU'RE KIDDING!

SOON THIS ARM WILL BE USELESS. AND IN THE END, MEWTWO'S CELLS WILL CONTROL MY ENTIRE BODY...AND TAKE MY LIFE.
GWRRRR
ALAS, A BACKWASH OF RENEGADE MEWTWO CELLS FOUND THEIR WAY UP INTO MY ARM...

...BUT WHEN I AM GONE, THERE WILL BE NO HOPE!
FOR THE MOMENT, I AM A LIVING MEWTWO LOCATOR...

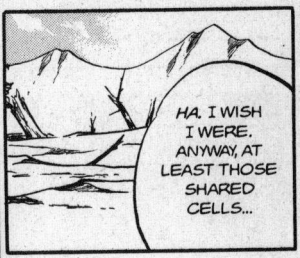
HA. I WISH I WERE. ANYWAY, AT LEAST THOSE SHARED CELLS...

...ENABLE US BOTH TO KNOW WHEN THE OTHER IS CLOSE. CALL IT A RESONANCE EFFECT... OR A NATURAL TRACKING DEVICE!
TWIK

WHAT SHOULD I FEAR NOW ?!!
LET TEAM ROCKET CALL ME A TRAITOR! LET THEM HOUND ME TO THE ENDS OF THE EARTH!
GWOOOO
HAAAAA!!
EEP!
KWRR
?
HEH... BUT I DO DRONE ON AND ON, DON'T I...?
KRAKLE KRAKLE
WHAT... ?!
DON'T BE STUPID! YOU CAN'T DO THIS ALONE!
I HAVE NO RIGHT TO DRAG YOU INTO THIS!
A FIREBALL WALL! YOU'LL BE SAFE INSIDE!

LISTEN, KID. THIS ISN'T ANOTHER ONE OF YOUR FUN ADVENTURES. IF I'M TOO LATE, CITY AFTER CITY WILL BE DESTROYED.
WHO'S STUPID ?!
JABB
THROB THROB
WRAAAGH !!
YOU'LL BE A GREAT TRAINER, RED... SOMEDAY!
PAT PAT
BLAINE... NO!!

35 And Mewtwo... Three!

HOOOO
KRAK
NGH !
B-SHOOOOOM
FFFFFF
AND THE FIREBALL WALL...
TP
THE TWISTER! IT'S... GONE?!
UNHHH...
HANG IN THERE, BLAINE !
BLAINE !
DOMP

WHAT ABOUT... THE T-TORNADO... AND MEWTWO...?
BLOWN AWAY... GONE!

YOU COULD HAVE GOTTEN YOURSELF KILLED!
HEH... YEAH... I GUESS...

PHEW
THEN... IT'S DONE!

RED.... DO YOU KNOW WHAT THIS IS?
M
IT'S...A MASTER BALL!

YEAH, BUT STILL...

MEWTWO'S POWER HAS GROWN SO GREAT THAT IT'S NEARLY IMPOSSIBLE TO GET CLOSE TO IT NOW.
BUT YOU SAW THE POWER OF THAT TORNADO.
FWOOO

THAT'S WHAT I THOUGHT... ONCE.
YOU SHOULD HAVE USED IT! WITH THAT THING, YOU DIDN'T HAVE TO RISK YOUR LIFE LIKE THAT!

!
YOUR EYES HAVE THE SAME COMPASSION IN THEM AS WHEN I FIRST MET YOU AT TEAM ROCKET'S HEADQUARTERS!
HA! RED, YOU HAVEN'T CHANGED A BIT!

...IN THE RESEARCH FACILITY CONSTRUCTED IN THE BASEMENT OF THE CELADON CITY GAME CENTER.
AS YOU CAN SEE, WE ARE CREATING MEWTWO FROM THE MEW CELL YOU RECOVERED...
BECAUSE I WAS THERE, KID! HA!
HOW... HOW'D YOU KNOW I WAS THERE...?

I HAD NO QUALMS ABOUT USING POKÉMON—EEVEE, GYARADOS—AS LABORATORY SUBJECTS.
I'D ALREADY THROWN AWAY MY POSITION AS A GYM LEADER TO JOIN TEAM ROCKET, HAVING FALLEN PREY TO MY... SCIENTIFIC CURIOSITY.

BUT YOU WERE DIFFERENT.
YOU MADE AN ALLY OUT OF GYARADOS, WHO HAD LOST TRUST IN HUMANS AFTER BEING USED IN EXPERIMENTS.
WHEN YOU LEARNED THAT A MEW WAS TO BE USED IN THE CREATION OF A MAN-MADE POKÉMON, YOU PROTECTED THAT MEW FROM JYNX.

YOU'RE THE REASON I TURNED AGAINST TEAM ROCKET! YOU'RE THE SOURCE OF MY STRENGTH AND COURAGE!
...
SEEING YOU TREAT POKÉMON AS PRECIOUS CREATURES... THE LOVE AND RESPECT YOU HAD FOR THEM...
...MADE ME ASHAMED OF WHAT I'D BECOME. I HAD SET OUT TO CREATE A FEROCIOUS BEAST...
...AND I SUCCEEDED! BUT THE BEAST WAS ME!

HOOOOOO
YOU'RE THE REASON... THERE WILL BE NO MORE VICTIMS OF MEWTWO...

FFFT

BLAINE... DON'T LEAVE ME NOW!
...

PANG
!!

NO...
NOBBLE
KLATTA
WAAAAA!!
HE'S HURT BAD. I DON'T DARE MOVE HIM...
BLAINE...
SHAA
IT'S... STILL ALIVE ?!
ARGH!!
KCH
BUT... HOW ?!
I HAVE TO FIND MEWTWO'S WEAK SPOT...
SHMM
GRRRN
SHUMP

GLEEEM
BOM
POLIWRATH! ATTACK!
WAK!
KONG
C-CAREFUL... THAT'S MEWTWO'S BATTLE PATTERN...
A SPOON?! WHAT KIND OF AN ATTACK IS THAT?!
VRRR
WRR
...BUT, ACTUALLY, THE PSYCHIC'S ULTIMATE WEAPON !!
FOR A SINGLE ENEMY...IT FORMS THAT SPOON-SHAPED WEAPON. SILLY LOOKING, PERHAPS...
HOOOO
IT ADAPTS ITS POWER TO ANY SITUATION...
FOR MULTIPLE ENEMIES...IT CHANNELS ITS ENERGY INTO A TORNADO...
GLEEEM

VOOSH
NOTHING IN NATURE CAN EQUAL IT!
MEWTWO WAS GENETICALLY ENGINEERED FOR COMBAT!
BWOK BWOK BWOK
D-GOOM
GYAH!!
AGH!
KRRRRM
...
THERE'S NOTHING TO BE DONE BUT... DESTROY IT!!
DON'T YOU SEE, RED?! YOU CAN'T WEAKEN IT! YOU CAN'T CATCH IT IN A POKÉ BALL!
KIIIIN
OKAY, THEN...

BOM
BOM
BOM
I'M COUNTING ON YOU GUYS!
THIS IS CRAZY, KID!
YOU'RE ONLY GOING TO MAKE THINGS WORSE !!
A GROUP ATTACK WILL JUST MAKE IT SHIFT BACK TO THE TORNADO!!
HOOOOO
NOW YOU'VE DONE IT! THE WIND'S RISING...!
FFFFFF
THEY'RE... THEY'RE ALL BEING BLOWN AWAY...
!
HOOOO

HOOOO
!
I JUST TRIED THAT... DIDN'T YOU SEE?!
RED... THAT'S IMPOSSIBLE!
I'VE GOTTA GET TO THE CENTER...
BEFORE THIS TWISTER GETS UP TO FULL POWER...
HOOOO
STOP, RED!
RRR
VWOOO
P-PIKACHU!
GLLLMP
RRRH!

?!
AWWP
MY... LORD...
?!
PFFF
GLLLMP
...

KLATTA
KLATTA
YEAH !!
KTOOOOW

BOOOF
ROLL

AS IT WAS FORMING THE TORNADO... YOU HIT IT WITH THE BALL?!
...

THERE WAS NO WAY I COULD'VE DONE THAT WHILE IT WAS HOLDING THE SPOON. I HAD TO LAUNCH A GROUP ATTACK TO GET IT TO SWITCH TO THE TWISTER.

RED... WHAT WAS THAT?!
OOOUCH.

!
OH HEY. HERE YOU GO, BLAINE.

BUT IT'S BEEN HELD PRISONER IN A LAB ITS WHOLE LIFE. ALL IT KNOWS ABOUT HUMANS IS THAT WE'RE CRUEL AND ARROGANT.
MEWTWO'S A PRETTY SCARY CREATURE, ALL RIGHT.

HEY, GUYS! GREAT JOB!
VOOOOM

FIND OUT, BLAINE. TEACH IT.
BUT WHAT IF IT LEARNS SOMETHING DIFFERENT...? WHAT IF IT SEES THAT NOT ALL HUMANS TREAT OTHER CREATURES BADLY?

OH... I JUST REMEMBERED SOMETHING I HAVEN'T THOUGHT OF IN A LONG WHILE.
SOMETHING THAT USED TO SUM UP EVERYTHING I ASPIRED TO...

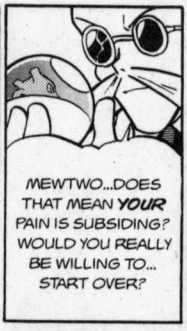
MEWTWO...DOES THAT MEAN YOUR PAIN IS SUBSIDING? WOULD YOU REALLY BE WILLING TO... START OVER?

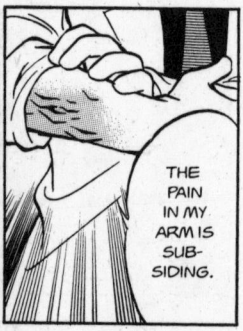
THE PAIN IN MY ARM IS SUB-SIDING.

SOMEONE WHO SPENDS HIS LIFE WITH, TRUSTS, AND IS TRUSTED BY HIS POKÉMON. SOMEONE LIKE YOU, RED.
THE WORDS... "POKÉMON TRAINER."

I'LL TAKE YOU ON ANYTIME– WHEN YOU'RE ALL BETTER!
SURE THING!
OH NO... I WAS JUST THINKING IT MIGHT BE FUN TO HAVE A TRAINER BATTLE SOMETIME...
OOOOF!
YOU SAY SOMETHING, BLAINE...?
ZOOM
OKAY, GUYS! WE'RE OFF TO INDIGO PLATEAU!

VIRIDIAN FOREST...
KSSH
gulp
!
OH NO... I'M LOST !
OWOOOOOOOO
WWIP
SSSHHHH
WHMMMM
EEVAAAAA!!

VSSSH
BNG 36 Drat That Dratini!
VSSHH
-WHIP !!
OKAY, VENUSAUR... VINE-
GNNNG
ARE YOU OKAY? ARE YOU HURT?!
YEAH... THANKS.
YOU SHOULD BE MORE CAREFUL OUT HERE! SURE YOU'RE OKAY?
BA-LUMP
WHEW !

WOW, YOU'RE SO LUCKY! I WISH I HAD A FRIEND LIKE THAT!
UH-HUH. DON'T LET IT SCARE YOU. VENUSAUR'S AS GENTLE AS THEY COME!
IS THAT YOURS ?!
AND THROW IT AT THAT RATTATA— THE WAY I JUST DID!
HMM... OKAY, THEN! TAKE THIS POKÉ BALL...
TOK TOK
NO.
YOU DON'T HAVE ANY POKÉMON OF YOUR OWN?
BOM
!!
FNN
LIKE THIS... ?!
"THUNDER-SHOCK" ?
CHK
C'MON— TRY GIVING PIKA A COMMAND. THIS ATTACK, F'RINSTANCE...
I'D LIKE YOU TO MEET PIKACHU— AN ELECTRIC-TYPE POKÉMON! THIS ONE'S NICKNAMED "PIKA."

BZZT BZZT BZZT
BZZT
PIKACHU... THUNDER-SHOCK !!
FIDGET FIDGET
GLEEM
O-OKAY...
YEAH! AND HURRY—PIKA'S WAITING !!
NOW! THROW THE POKÉ BALL AT IT!
WOBBLE WOBBLE
OKAY... WE DEFEATED THE LAST ONE, BUT THIS ONE WE'LL JUST WEAKEN... AND THEN...
WOW! YOU CAN TELL PIKA'S HAPPY TO BE BACK IN ITS HOME FOREST!
OOH... NICE TO MEET YOU, RATTATA !!
YOU CAPTURED IT! THAT MEANS YOU'RE RESPONSIBLE FOR IT—AND IT'LL DO WHATEVER YOU SAY!
IT'S IN THE BALL!!
BOM
FOOON
HYAH!!
...AND IT'LL FIT RIGHT IN YOUR POCKET !!
DOESN'T MATTER HOW BIG A POKÉMON IS, THE POKÉ BALL WILL SHRINK IT DOWN...

WHOOOO OOOO

WILD POKÉMON AREN'T USUALLY SO... SAVAGE!!
SOME-THING STRANGE IS GOING ON THOUGH...

IT'S OKAY. DON'T BE A-FRAID.
WHAT'S G-GOING ON ...?!!

RUN !!

GROOOOARR
AAAAH !!
EEEEK !!

BOM

KCH
SHOOT !!

HERE TOO ?!
SHHP

WHEW...
?!
?!
PFF
PFF
PFF

FLAP
FLAP
HEH HEH HEH.
WHEN THINGS ARE COMING AT YOU FROM ALL DIRECTIONS... THE ONLY WAY TO GO IS UP!!

HWOOSH
OKAY, THEN— VIRIDIAN CITY IT IS!

SO WHERE DO YOU LIVE, KID?
VIRIDIAN CITY.

ANOTHER THING THAT'S WEIRD... THAT DRATINI SHOULDN'T EVEN BE IN THE FOREST! AND WHY DID THEY ALL ATTACK AT ONCE?
WHAT'S HAP-PENING...?

DO YOU KNOW HOW WORRIED WE--?!
?
I TOLD YOU TO STAY OUT OF THE FOREST! WEIRD THINGS HAVE BEEN HAPPENING IN THERE!
WHERE WERE YOU?!
VIRIDIAN CITY...
DOZENS OF POKÉMON HAVE BEEN APPEARING ALL OF A SUDDEN--INCLUDING TYPES WE'VE NEVER SEEN BEFORE!
WHAT DO YOU MEAN, "WEIRD THINGS"?!
WHAT'S THAT?!
CHK
HMM... WHAT'S GOING ON IN THE VIRIDIAN FOREST...?
...THE FAMOUS POKÉMON EXPERT OF PALLET TOWN?!
YOU MEAN THE PROFESSOR OAK...
YEP!
A POKÉDEX!
I'M ON A QUEST TO FILL THIS POKÉDEX WITH INFORMATION ABOUT POKÉMON. IT'S A GIFT FROM PROFESSOR OAK!

I'M LOOKING FOR OTHER TRAINERS TO BATTLE ALONG THE WAY SO I CAN BECOME THE ULTIMATE POKÉMON MASTER!!
MY NAME'S RED. I'M FROM PALLET TOWN TOO. I'M ON MY WAY TO INDIGO PLATEAU.

THE GYM'S BEEN CLOSED FOR A LONG TIME. AND THE GYM LEADER DISAPPEARED.
HUH? WHY NOT?

OH... WELL, I'M SORRY TO SAY... THIS TOWN DOESN'T HAVE ANYONE WHO COULD GIVE YOU A DECENT MATCH.

INVIN-CIBLE, HUH?
HMM

THEY SAY HE WAS INVINCIBLE– THAT NO ONE COULD DEFEAT HIM... BUT NOW HE'S GONE...
Viridian City
GYM
NO ONE EVEN KNOWS WHO HE REALLY WAS.

ACROSS THE RIVER? GOT IT!!
KGGK

WHICH WAY IS THIS GYM?!
HUH? HUH?
IT'S ACROSS THE RIVER, BUT...

BOM
!!

DON'T BE SCARED !!
WHOA! IT'S OKAY!!

IT'S HUGE !!
EEE-YAAA !!

POKÉMON CAN BE SCARY...BUT THEY'RE BASICALLY KIND, LOVING CREATURES.
LISTEN TO ME... PLEASE...

...THEN THEY'LL ALWAYS BE YOUR FRIENDS. DO YOU GET WHAT I'M SAYING?
BUT IF YOU RAISE THEM WITH KINDNESS AND GENTLE-NESS...

...THEN THEY'LL GROW UP TO BE BAD TOO.
IF THEIR OWNERS ARE BAD AND TRAIN THEIR POKÉMON TO DO BAD THINGS...

OKAY, THEN– LET'S GO!
W-WAIT! THE BRIDGE IS WAY OVER–
GOOD. AS LONG AS YOU REMEMBER THAT, YOU'LL BE ON THE RIGHT SIDE!
I DO.
THANKS !!
HYAAAH!!
POM
SHWRRLLL
RETURN !!
AMAZING...
GASP
...
PWAP
SEE YA LATER !

AT THE GYM...
Viridian City
GYM
VIRIDIAN GYM CLOSED
OKAY... THIS IS THE PLACE!
DIGG
HERE...
BOM
...SCOPING OUT A PLACE LIKE THIS!
CHK
VENUSAUR'S VINE IS PERFECT FOR...
FIRST LET'S TAKE A LOOK AROUND THE OUTSIDE...
SHLRRR SHLRRR
VENUSAUR !!

I'VE GOT TO FIND OUT WHAT'S GOING ON HERE!
THE INVINCIBLE MISSING GYM LEADER...
THIS IS THE PLACE WHERE PROF. OAK AND I LOOKED FOR YOU! LOOKS LIKE IT'S BEEN CLOSED EVER SINCE...
VIRIDIAN GYM
CLOSED

HEY! WAIT !!
GUESS WE'D BETTER GO INSI... HUH ?!
BUT THERE AREN'T ANY CLUES...TO ANYTHING!

OOOOOM
GASP
KRIII
WHOA... IT'S PITCH-DARK.

!
SOME-ONE'S THERE !!

VIRIDIAN GYM LEADER... UMMM...
CAN'T READ THE NAME... IT'S BROKEN OFF.
...
VIRIDIAN GYM LEADER
NNI
BUT WHERE ?!
BUT I HAVE A FEELING I'VE SEEN THIS FACE SOME-WHERE BEFORE...
V-VENUSAUR!! WHAT IS IT?!
GNG
GNG
POP
?!

YOU CAME...AS I EXPECTED YOU WOULD. WELCOME TO THE VIRIDIAN CITY GYM.
ZSH

I'VE WAITED A LONG TIME FOR YOU...RED OF PALLET TOWN!
WHO ARE Y-YOU ?!

HOW DOES HE KNOW MY NAME?!

hwph

JRRR
WHAT IS IT WITH THIS GUY...?!

Viridian City
GYM
VIRIDIAN GYM CLOSED

AN EXPERT, EVEN...?
LOOK AT YOU... YOU MUST BE A FAIRLY EXPERIENCED TRAINER BY NOW...

TMM
WHO ARE YOU?!
YOU'VE BEEN ON THIS MISSION TO COMPLETE OAK'S POKÉDEX FOR SOME TIME NOW.
YOU MUST HAVE DEFEATED QUITE A FEW GYM LEADERS IN THE PROCESS!

!

SSSS
WAS YOUR LAST VICTORY THE TIME YOU WENT FOSSIL HUNTING IN DIGLETT'S CAVE...? NO, IT WAS WHEN THE SILPH COMPANY HEADQUARTERS WAS CRUMBLING...

C'MON, MISTER! WHAT'S TAKING YOU SO LONG?!
YOU'R JUST BUNDLE ENER AREN YOU, RE HEH.
IT... CAN'T BE... !!
WHERE WOULD IT GO...?
I CAN'T SHAKE THIS FEELING THAT...I'VE SEEN YOU SOMEWHERE BEFORE...
WHAT IS IT?
UMMM.
GOSH.
I CAN'T REMEM-BER WHERE, BUT...
ARE YOU SURE YOU DON'T REMEMBER ME?
HOOOSH
LOOK OUT, MISTE !
MMM ?
THE FOSSIL GUY...?!

HMMM
THE SAND IS HITTING THEM BUT IT ONLY SEEMS TO ANNOY THEM. WHAT ARE YOU GOING TO DO NOW?
...WHY DON'T YOU TAKE ONE? AS A FAREWELL.
SNEER
VIP
HA HA HA! THAT'S RIGHT.
WHEN I MET YOU IN PEWTER CITY...
HAHAHA
I WAS THE VIRIDIAN GYM LEADER.

YOU'VE CLASHED WITH TEAM ROCKET MANY TIMES. NOW YOU HAVE THE HONOR OF MEETING ITS *LEADER!*

FROM NOW ON, YOU CAN CALL ME... *GIOVANNI!*

37 Golly, Golem!

SO DO I STRIKE FIRST? OR IS THAT SUICIDE...?
ARE WE THE ONLY TWO IN THE GYM?! NAH... IT CAN'T BE! HE'S GOT TO HAVE HIS UNDERLINGS SOMEWHERE AROUND HERE!
DON'T WORRY. THERE'S NO ONE HERE BUT YOU AND ME. I HAVE NO REASON TO LIE.
Viridian City
GYM
AND YOU'RE DEBATING WHETHER IT WOULD BE WISE TO STRIKE FIRST.
...
I SEE YOU ARE WONDERING HOW MANY OF YOUR ENEMIES ARE IN THE BUILDING. YOU'RE TRYING TO ASSESS HOW POWERFUL I AM...
!!
TAK
TAK
TAK
TAK
TAK
KWRR
NOT ONLY THAT...
BWOOF
?!

I'M EVEN UNARMED... YOU HAVE ME AT QUITE A DISADVANTAGE... HEH.
NOW. COME AT ME WITH ALL YOU'VE GOT.

BOM
...WOULDN'T BE MAKING FUN OF ME, WOULD YOU?!

YOU...

?!
FSH
VNN

DOP
WHA—?!

FANNNNNG
!!

SSSHHHH
IT TOOK ONE SECOND FOR YOU TO GRAB YOUR POKÉ BALL.

WHAT... JUST... HAP-PENED...?!

THREE SECONDS ELAPSED BY THE TIME POLIWRATH LEFT THE BALL AND BEGAN ATTACKING.
VAN

BY THE TIME YOU THREW IT, ANOTHER SECOND PASSED.

MORE THAN ENOUGH TIME TO REACH THE POKÉ BALLS ON THE FLOOR AND LAUNCH A COUNTER-ATTACK...
...FOR ME, AT LEAST.

IT'S A SHAME, RED... IT REALLY IS.
YOU DISSIN' ME?

MOST PEOPLE SEEM TO THINK THAT THE MARK OF GOOD TRAINERS IS SIMPLY THEIR COMMAND OF POKÉMON.
BUT THE TRAINER'S OWN POWER, SKILL... AND SPEED... ARE JUST AS ESSENTIAL.

HUH...?
DON'T MISUNDERSTAND.

SST SST SST
FWOOOO
I COULD USE A TRAINER WITH YOUR STUBBORNNESS, YOUR EXPLOSIVE ENERGY, YOUR EMPATHY FOR POKÉMON...
...I CAN KNOCK 'EM OFF THEIR FEET!!
THE SHAME... IS THAT YOU'RE NOT ON MY SIDE.
THERE WAS NOTHING SHAMEFUL ABOUT YOUR ATTACK.

YOU THINK I'D JOIN YOU?!
AT FIRST, I THOUGHT NOTHING OF THEM. BUT THEN I KEPT HEARING ABOUT THE SAME YOUNG MAN SCORING VICTORY AFTER VICTORY...
I'VE HEARD ABOUT YOUR BATTLES WITH MY CAPTAINS.

SO... HOW ABOUT A BET?
YOUR INDEPENDENCE AND HONOR ARE AMONG THE TRAITS I ADMIRE IN YOU.
WHRR
NO, ACTUALLY... I DON'T.

...
ON THE OTHER HAND, YOU HAVE FIVE POKÉMON STILL AT YOUR SIDE.
IT WOULD TAKE SIX SECONDS FOR ME TO SEIZE ONE AND ATTACK.
AS YOU CAN SEE, MY POKÉMON ARE ON THE FLOOR AND FAR FROM ME.

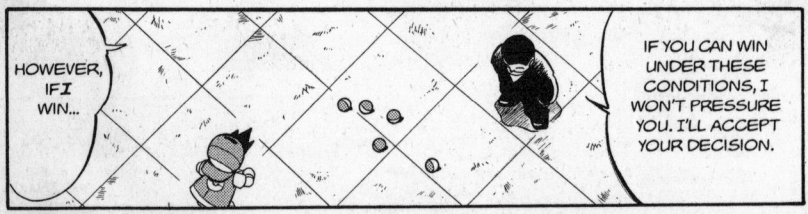
HOWEVER, IF I WIN...
IF YOU CAN WIN UNDER THESE CONDITIONS, I WON'T PRESSURE YOU. I'LL ACCEPT YOUR DECISION.

WELL? DOES YOUR SILENCE SIGNIFY ASSENT? OR ARE YOU JUST AFRAID?
...YOU WILL SPEND THE REST OF YOUR LIFE BATTLING FOR ME AT MY SIDE!

HA HA HA HA! THAT'S WHAT I LOOK FOR IN A LIEUTENANT!
BUT ONLY IF IT'S A FAIR FIGHT!
AFRAID?!! I DON'T THINK SO! I ACCEPT YOUR CHALLENGE!
TOK

VSH
VSH
A FAIR FIGHT MEANS...MY BEST AGAINST YOUR BEST!
LET'S GO!
KCH
SHP
GOFF
BOM
I BEAT YOU, GIOVANNI !
SNORR
MEGA PUNCH !!

WHOK
?!
BUT A GREAT TRAINER KNOWS WHEN TO LET HIS OPPONENT STRIKE FIRST SO AS TO...
YOU'RE FAST ALL RIGHT, RED...
SNAG
...USE HIS SPEED AGAINST HIM!
BBOM
WHAT THE...?!
GKOOOM
NO!
VNNN
GOLLL
!
LEARN SOME-THING!
BOM
PAY ATTENTION!
I BEAT YOU WITH MY SPEED BEFORE—NOW I'LL BEAT YOU WITH YOUR OWN!

GOLLLL
ACK!
GOLL
GAAH!
TM
TM
TM
TM
...
HEH HEH HEH... WHAT'S YOUR NEXT MOVE, RED?
DON'T PANIC! THINK !!
SH-SHOOT... !
OKAY, THEN...
GOLEM'S BOUNCING LIKE A PINBALL, TRYING TO HONE IN ON THE SPOT WHERE MY NEXT POKÉMON'S GONNA APPEAR!
GOLEM'S... LIKE SOME KINDA PROJECTILE BALL!

GOLEM! ATTACK!
SHHH
HEH
WHAT IF I DON'T TAKE OUT ANOTHER POKÉMON?!
...GOLEM'S BOUND TO GET SICK OF SEARCHING... AND HEAD FOR THAT HOLE IN THE WALL!
IF I JUST LET IT KEEP BOUNCING...
GOLLL
DOMP!
SNORLAX!
AND THE SECOND IT DOES—
SNOR?

SH-BAMMM
A HEAD...
...BUTT !!
HOW SAD. GOLEM'S CRUMBLING! TOO BAD...
KRRRMMMMM
HOW'S THAT FOR A HARD HEAD ?!
LOOK OUT FOR THE... !
SNOR-LAX !
...ITS BEST ATTACK INVOLVES SHAT-TERING!
P-P-P-P AMMMM
AND NOW...
BOOM BA BOOM BA
NO !
ROCK THROW !

S-SNORLAX!
KRAK
DOMM
EXPLOSION!!
TINK
TOO LATE, RED. IT'S OVER.
SSHHH
WHICH IS WHY I LET THE FIGHT MOVE OUTSIDE.
THE MOMENT YOU PICKED SNORLAX, I CHOSE EXPLOSION FOR MY FINAL ATTACK. BUT EXPLOSION CAN'T BE USED INDOORS.
ONE MOVE AND BEEDRILL DRILLS YOU.
I TOLD YOU YOU'D LEARN FROM ME!

GNNG
POOF
...
BZZZZ
NOW... DON'T YOU THINK IT'S ABOUT TIME TO GIVE UP?
...
KCHK
WELL, RED...?
FLAP
...IT'S TIME FOR YOU TO GIVE UP!

FWAP
AERODACTYL !
YOU HAD A POKÉ BALL UNDER YOUR FOOT!
FFFSH
HAAAAA !!
38 Long Live the Nidoqueen?!
KRAK
HYPER BEAM !
THIS BATTLE'S NOT OVER YET!
DID WE DO IT ?!
FFF FFF
FFF
XXXXSSSSHHH
GAH!

SSSHHHHHHH
THEY'RE... GONE ?!
?!
GRRRM MM
!!
TH-THAT HOLE... !!
NO WAY !
VSSH
TMP
GR RR ROOOOM MM
EARTHQUAKE! THE GYM'S GONNA COLLAPSE!
KRASH
NKH!
VVM
NO! P-POLI– !!

SHHHHHHHH
Viridian
TOOOOOM
NIDO... KING...?!
ZMM!
KH.. KHUH...
HEH... I'M IMPRESSED, RED.
STOMP
HUF
HUF
TH-THAT'S WHAT CAUSED THIS QUAKE?!
SO FAR I'VE BEEN USING POKÉMON OUTSIDE OF MY SPECIALTY—LIKE CLOYSTER AND BEEDRILL...
BUT YOU'RE ACTUALLY FORCING ME TO USE MY BEST FIGHTERS!

VOON
RHYHORN! TAIL WHIP!
UH
NNGH! AERO-DACTYL!

SO MUCH FOR YOUR OVER-HEAD ESCAPE...
DOMF
RHYYY
NO!

NGH!
GRIP
KRAAAK
RHYDON! FISSURE!
NOW IT'S TIME TO TRAP THE TRAINER!
YAAAH!!
DESTROY THE OPPO-NENT'S FOOTING... A GOOD TRICK TO REMEM-BER.
KRRRRMM
KRMBL

YOU'RE A CLEVER ONE—CHOOSING YOUR
I CREATED THE LIGHT SCREEN AROUND SAFFR
YOU'VE FOUGHT AGAINST QUITE A FEW GYM LEADERS, EACH WITH THEIR OWN SPECIALTY...THE "ELECTRIC" LT. SURGE... THE "POISONOUS" KOGA...THE "PSYCHIC" SABRINA...
AND NOW ME...THE MASTER OF "GROUND" POKÉMON!
LT. SURGE, ONE THIRD OF THE HAND
STARE
!!
NIDO-QUEEN...
NIDO-KING!
DUGTRIO... RHYDON... RHYHORN...
YOU KNOW OF MY PROWESS, DON'T YOU?
THE GEMS OF THE VIRIDIAN CITY GYM!
AND ME WITHOUT MY POKÉ BALLS... ALL LOST IN THE RUBBLE!
SAID TO BE THE GREATEST OF THEM ALL!
GIO-VANNI... THE MISSING GYM LEAD-ER...

USSH
GO !!
IT'S CRUMBLING!
GLINT
WAP
PAP
DIG
DIG
WHAT ?!
MY ATTACK SHATTERED THE OPENING MECHANISM OF YOUR POKÉ BALLS. YOUR POKÉMON CANNOT BE RELEASED.
KRAACK
DUG-TRIO...?!
YOU FOUGHT WELL, RED. YOU TRAVELED THROUGHOUT THIS LAND AND SURVIVED CHALLENGES THAT NO ONE IMAGINED YOU COULD. BUT YOU NEVER REALIZED...
OHHH...
SLUMP

TO YOU, THEY SEEMED TO BE UNCONNECTED INCIDENTS... BUT ALL OF YOUR BATTLES WERE PIECES OF ONE GREAT PLAN!
...
...THAT EVERY PLACE YOU VISITED AND FOUGHT... WAS ALREADY UNDER MY CONTROL!
ALL OF THE POKÉMON WE COLLECTED FOR EXPERIMENTAL PURPOSES WERE BROUGHT TO CELADON CITY LABS FOR BIO-MODIFI-CATION...
...THEN PUT THROUGH BATTLE TRAINING IN THE NEIGHBORING TOWN OF SAFFRON CITY...
S.S.ANNE
NEXT, THEY WERE TAKEN TO VIRIDIAN CITY VIA CINNABAR ISLAND...THEN ON TO VERMILION CITY TO BE PUT ABOARD THE S.S. ANNE.
TRANSFER HAD TO BE ACCOMPLISHED BY SEA BECAUSE THE NORTHERN HIGHWAYS WERE BEING WATCHED BY THE "GOOD" GYM LEADERS OF THOSE CITIES.
TMPTMP
AFTER ALL, WITH THE VIRIDIAN GYM LEADER "MISSING," NO TRAINERS EVER CAME HERE LOOKING FOR A BATTLE! SO I'VE HAD ALL THE PRIVACY I NEEDED TO DEVELOP AN UNSTOPPABLE ARMY OF POKÉMON!
AND FINALLY THEY WERE BROUGHT TO THE BREEDING GROUND WHERE THESE EXPERIMENTAL ANIMALS REGAINED THEIR PRIMAL, SAVAGE POWERS. HERE—IN THE VAST DEPTHS OF THE VIRIDIAN FOREST!

I CAN'T AFFORD TO LOSE!
GRR
I'M THE ONLY ONE WHO KNOWS ABOUT HIS EVIL PLAN... AND NOW I'M THE ONLY ONE WHO CAN STOP HIM!
PIKACHU!! GOOD GOING!!
PAP
!!
VWING
KRAK
LET'S DO IT!!
GNG
THIS IS A BATTLE TO STOP TEAM ROCKET!
AND I'M GONNA WIN!!
WOBBLE
GIO-VANNI!!
THIS ISN'T JUST A BATTLE AGAINST A GYM LEADER ANYMORE!!

YOUR LAST POKÉMON IS PIKACHU! ITS GREATEST WEAPON—THUNDERBOLT!
VMM
...HOW THIS WILL END!
HA HA HA HA! YOU HAVEN'T CHANGED A BIT SINCE THE LAST TIME I SAW YOU, RED! HEH... LET ME TELL YOU...
...THEN ANOTHER TWO SECONDS FOR THE ATTACK TO REACH ME. BY THE TIME THOSE FIVE SECONDS HAVE ELAPSED...
...TWO SECONDS TO CHARGE ENOUGH ENERGY FOR THE THUNDER BOLT...
IT WILL TAKE ONE SECOND FOR THE POKÉ BALL TO OPEN AND FOR PIKACHU TO EMERGE...
NIIIIII
...NIDO-QUEEN WILL HAVE PIERCED YOU WITH ITS POISON STING!
NIDO-QUEEN, ATTACK!!
FWAAA
GOT ALL THE ANSWERS, DO YOU?!!

BZZT BZZT
!
TIME REMAINING
4
SECONDS
TIME REMAINING
5
SECONDS
BZZZT BZZZT
BOM
THUNDER-BOLT!
KKAKKAKKAKKAKK

FLICK
TIME REMAINING
2
SECONDS
PIII
TIME REMAINING
3
SECONDS
ZZZZZZZZZ
NO!! THAT'S IMPOSSIBLE-!!
ZZZAK

TAP
HUF HUF
IF PIKACHU DOESN'T HAVE TIME TO CHARGE UP AFTER I OPEN THE POKÉ BALL...
THOMP
NO ONE CAN HOLD A POKÉ BALL LACED WITH THOUSANDS OF VOLTS OF ELECTRICITY...!!
TOPPLE
N... NO...!!
...THEN IT'LL JUST HAVE TO CHARGE UP INSIDE THE POKÉ BALL!
IT'S TEAM ROCKET'S!
SNAP
THAT GLOVE!!
PAT
NOPE. YOUR DOWN-FALL...
...WAS ONE OF MY OWN... WEAP-ONS...
DOMM
C...CAN'T BELIEVE... THAT MY DOWN-FALL...
GOK

FUNK
WOBBLE
...
...WAS THE SUFFERING OF THE POKÉMON YOU TRIED TO CORRUPT FOR YOUR EVIL PURPOSES!
YOU'RE ALIVE !!
BLINK
HUH...? WHERE A-AM...?
EVERYONE'S GOING INTO THE FOREST NOW TO CALM THE POKÉMON THAT WERE ACTING UP.
TEE HEE... WE FINALLY GOT UP THE NERVE TO DO SOME-THING...
THE FOREST?! WHAT ABOUT ALL THE POKÉMON?! THE ONES THAT WERE ACTING STRANGE?!
FSH
HUH?
YOU FAINTED AT THE EDGE OF THE FOREST! I WAS AFRAID—

AND... WELL... SEE...
OUR GYM... THEY SAY IT GOT DESTROYED IN SOME HUGE BATTLE...
WHAT?
UMMM...
BUT SOMETHIN' TELLS ME THEY'LL NEED MY HELP!
OOOF!
ALL RIGHT!
UH-HUH.
Y'MEAN... ME?
NOBODY AROUND HERE IS VERY GOOD WITH POKÉMON... SO WE WERE THINKING THAT IT MIGHT BE NICE TO HAVE SOMEONE AROUND TO...YOU KNOW... TEACH US?
IT WOULD BE AN HONOR!
AFTER I'VE ACHIEVED ENOUGH TO BE A TRUE GYM LEADER! WHEN I COME BACK...
...I'LL BE THE BEST GYM LEADER EVER!
WAIT FOR ME!

YAMMER YAMMER YAMMER
SINGLE LINE, PLEASE... FORM A SINGLE LINE...

TOSS
HEY, OLD MAN! NO CUTTING!

CUT!
WOO HOO
'SCUSE ME!!

WADDLE WADDLE
OOOO! NOW ISN'T THIS SOMETHING!

EH?!
HUFF HUFF
IS THAT HOW YOU TREAT YOUR ELDERS?!

POINK
!!

PLEASE GIVE THAT BACK! IT'S MINE!
WHERE IS THE OWNER OF THIS POKÉMON?! THE "POKÉMON LOVERS CLUB" WILL DECLARE YOU AN HONORARY MEMBER ON THE SPOT!
FLAPPA

39 Just a Spearow Carrier

GROWRR
BOING
BWOK
GOTCHA !!
SSSS
DOUBLE TEAM !
SHLK
PING
ALL RIGHT!! I'M IN THE SEMI-FINALS!
GROUP "C" 1ST PLACE RED
FNSH
?
YOU EVER SEE A BATTLE THAT INTENSE BEFORE?!
OOOO!

ROOOAR
HOOHOO
YAAAY

YOU...
!

HEY
!

PING
GROUP "D"
1ST PLACE BLUE
WINNER OF THE "D" GROUP... BLUE!

?
TUP

WAFFT

YEAH ?
...EVERY SINGLE WINNER OF THE CHAMPIONSHIPS HAS BEEN A TRAINER FROM PALLET TOWN.
CHK
I DON'T SUPPOSE I NEED TO TELL YOU, RED, THAT IN THE HISTORY OF THE POKÉMON LEAGUE...
THE QUESTION THIS YEAR IS WHICH ONE WILL IT BE...
PAP
HWRRRRRRR
POM
HEH
YEAH. YOU... OR ME?
GROUP WINNERS, PLEASE PROCEED TO THE ARENA!
I'M LOOKING FORWARD TO BATTLING YOU IN THE FINAL ROUND!

ZIP
HUH ?!
O-KAY!! LET'S GO!!

TEEHEE
THERE YOU ARE, MY LITTLE NIDO! OOOO, AND LOOK WHO FOUND A BOY-FRIEND! ♡

SMOOCH
OH MY !

WHAT... ?!
OUR POKÉMON LIKE EACH OTHER...SO WE SHOULD TOO! HOW ABOUT A POKÉMON TRADE TO SEAL THE DEAL, HMM? LIKE...MY WEEDLE FOR YOUR BIG, STRONG BUTTERFREE! ♡

WHADDYA MEAN, WHAT'S UP?! WHAT ARE YOU DOING IN—
I MEAN... HI, RED! WHAT'S UP?!

EEEK
YOU!! STILL UP TO YOUR TRICKS, I SEE !!

GROUP "A"
1ST PLACE GREEN
A
TEE-HEE!! ♡ WEREN'T THOSE PRELIM-INARIES A BREEZE ?
...!!
ping
POIK POIK
YOU'RE GONNA BE IN... THE SEMI-FINALS ?!
WELL...
USSH
SEE YOU IN THE ARENA ! ♡
I DON'T PLAN ON LOSING... CUZ I'M A TRAINER FROM PALLET TOWN TOO, Y'KNOW!
WHAT ?!
YOU'RE A... YOU'RE...
HEY! GET BACK HERE! WHAT DID YOU SAY?!
CONGRATS ON THEM PRELIMS THERE, FELLER!
PAP
THE FINAL FOUR! HOO-WEE !
Y'SEE THE MATCH-UPS YET?
BILL !

PLAYER GREEN
WINNER GROUP "A"
YOU MEAN IT'S ME AND BLUE IN THE FIRST ROUND?!
PLAYER RED
WINNER GROUP "C"
PLAYER BLUE
WINNER GROUP "D"

AH, HECK, RED!
SIGH ...

ROOOAR
AT THE FINAL STAGE ARENA...

SCARY LOOKIN' FELLA, AIN'T HE?
YEAH... HEY, THIS "B" WINNER, DR. O...

I KNOW YOU WAS FIGGERIN' ON COMIN' UP AGINST THAT RIVAL O' YOURS IN THE FINALS... BUT REAL LIFE DON'T FOLLOW A SCRIPT!

AND WEIRD...

GO NG
LET THE MATCH BEGIN !!
BOM
BOM
BUT WHAT'S WITH THAT GUY'S SPEAROW?!
SHE WOULDN'T LEAD WITH A CUTE POKÉMON UNLESS IT'S PART OF HER STRATEGY...PROBABLY TO GET HER OPPONENT TO LET DOWN HIS GUARD...
SHE'S BRINGING OUT A JIGGLYPUFF IN A MATCH LIKE THIS?!
HEY! THAT GIRL...
MURMUR MURMUR
...
OOOOO

BZZZZZ
WELL, LET'S FIND OUT, SHALL WE?
...
...JUST CUZ I'M A CUTE LI'L GIRL?
TSK! A SILLY OL' SPEAROW IN THE POKÉMON LEAGUE SEMIFINALS? YOU THINK I'M SOME KIND OF PUSHOVER...
BASH
ATTACK !!
TEE-HEE!♡ I WON ALL MY PRELIMS WITH A SINGLE SHOT!♡
SHOOOOOOOO
VOOSH
GRIN

DN DN DN DN DN
EEYAAAA !!
FURY ATTACK !!
HEY! NO FAIR! JIGGLYPUFF, SING!!
NNNGH... SO... SLEEPY... WHO'S NOT P-PLAYING FAIR...?!
UHHH
HH
JIGGLYPUFF DOESN'T HAVE THE SPEED TO FIGHT FLYING-TYPE POKÉMON!
THE SONG ISN'T REACHING THE SPEAROW.
FWAP

IDIOT! WHAT ARE YOU DOING?! SWITCH TO AN AERIAL BATTLE!
VSSH
VSSH
VSSH
OOH, YOU! TAKE THAT!! AND THAT!!

WHAT ?!
I CAN'T!! I DON'T HAVE ANY FLYING-TYPE POKÉMON, OKAY?!

WHAT ?!
...I CAN'T.

C'MON!! HURRY!!

THEY'RE ALL FLYING-TYPE POKÉMON! HE MUST KNOW GREEN'S WEAKNESS!

BOM
I THINK YOU MAY BE THE ONE WHO UNDER-ESTIMATED YOUR OPPONENT... "LI'L GIRL"!
BOM

...IS WRONG !
!!
LET THIS BE A LESSON TO YOU. STEALING...

SSHHH

HEH
WHO... WHO IS THIS GUY...?!
TING
WAWA WAWA MIWA
DISABLE!
AN OPENING!!
WELL, IF AN AERIAL BATTLE'S MY ONLY CHOICE...
KCH
BOM
BLASTOISE!! NOW!!
HUH?!
SHWNG
DUUUUMMM
KSSSH

IT MAY NOT BE WHAT YOU DEFINE AS "AERIAL"...
JUST CUZ I DON'T HAVE ANY FLYING-TYPE POKÉMON DOESN'T MEAN I CAN'T GET INTO THE AIR!
DUUUM
MM
HYDRO PUMP!
BLOO
OOSH
WHRRR
...BUT IT WORKS FOR ME!!
SHPLAAAAP
SLIP
OH, AND WHILE WE'RE AT IT... LET'S SEE WHAT YOU LOOK LIKE, SHALL WE?

AN AERIAL HYDRO PUMP! YOU SAW IT HERE FIRST!
SHPAPAPAPAPAPAPA
SLIP
HEH
THE MASK– IT'S SLIPPING OFF HIS FACE–!
BABABABABA
SSHUUUU
WELL, MY SPEAROW CAN'T DO THAT WITH WORDS, BUT...
?
YOU KNOW HOW A PARROT BOUNCES YOUR WORDS BACK AT YOU?

PZZZZZZZ
MIRROR MOVE !!
THE SPEAROW'S MAKIN' AN ENERGY REFLECTOR FIELD!!
IT'S REFLECTING!!
BLOOSH
EEEEP !!
BLOOSH
THWAP
BLASTOISE
HP
ITS HEALTH LEVELS...
UH-HUH...
N... NO...
ZZZMM
FLUTTERRRRRR

MURMUR
MURMUR
WHAT'S WRONG WITH HER?
BRRRRRRRR
D-DON'T COME NEAR ME!!
SIX YEARS AGO, A LITTLE GIRL OF FIVE WAS ABDUCTED BY A LARGE LEGENDARY BIRD POKÉMON...
BRRRRRRR
WHAT'S WRONG, GREEN? A PHOBIA OF FLYING-TYPE POKÉMON?!
I WAS DEEPLY INVOLVED WITH THE INVESTIGATION. I COULD NEVER FORGET HER FACE.
AT THE TIME, I HAD A GRANDSON OF THE SAME AGE, SO I FELT COMPELLED TO GET INVOLVED.
OOOO!
HEY...! THIS DR. O GUY...
THAT'S... THAT'S...
SLLLIP
IMAGINE MY SURPRISE WHEN MY SECURITY CAMERAS CAUGHT THAT VERY SAME GIRL... STEALING MY SQUIRTLE!

G-GET AWAY !!
SWSH
PROFES-SOR OAK!
IT'S NO SURPRISE THAT A TRAUMA LIKE THAT WOULD LEAVE YOU TERRIBLY AFRAID OF BIRDS, GREEN...

ACK!
POOOM
MIRROR MOVE !

BLOSH
BLAST-OISE !!
W-WATER GUN !!

TOMP
!!

YAAAAAAY
THE WINNER... DR. O !!

PING
HP:
!

WHY DID YOU DO IT?
NOW, YOUNG LADY... YOU OWE ME AN EXPLANATION. YOU DIDN'T HAVE TO STEAL POKÉMON.
TMP
I... LOST ?!
SO...THE SQUIRTLE THIEF...WAS YOU...!
THEN ONE DAY I FOUND OUT THAT TWO BOYS MY AGE—FROM PALLET TOWN—GOT A POKÉMON AND A POKÉDEX FROM PROFESSOR OAK AND STARTED THEIR TRAINING JOURNEYS!
I GREW UP IN A PLACE I DIDN'T KNOW... WITH NO FAMILY!
ALL I REMEMBERED WAS THAT I CAME FROM SOMEWHERE CALLED PALLET TOWN.
IT WASN'T FAIR !
I WANTED TO DO WHAT THEY WERE DOING !!
...WAS FROM PALLET TOWN TOO!!
GRRR
BUT I...

SHHHHH
I WANTED TO GET A POKÉMON FROM YOU...
... AND A POKÉDEX TO TAKE ON MY TRAINING JOURNEY!

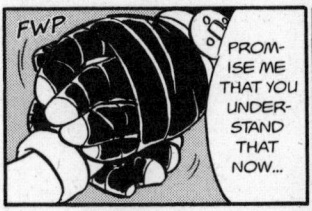
FWP
PROMISE ME THAT YOU UNDERSTAND THAT NOW...

SHP
GREEN... DO YOU REMEMBER WHAT I JUST SAID? STEALING IS WRONG...

OH...
HERE. THE THIRD POKÉDEX.
NOW YOU TOO ARE A TRAINER FROM PALLET TOWN.

HECK, I CAN RELATE TO BEIN' SNATCHED BY A LEGENDARY BIRD...
I GET IT.

I'M JUST GLAD YOU'RE ALL RIGHT.
THERE, THERE...
WAAAH!!

SNIG
I... PR-PR-PRO...

FAN FAN
WHEW! WHAT A WORKOUT! HAVEN'T SWEATED LIKE THAT IN A WHILE!
IN THE PLAYER LOCKER ROOM...
NO... I'VE ALREADY WON MYSELF A CHAMPIONSHIP. I DON'T NEED THIS.
...THAT WHOEVER WINS THE MATCH BETWEEN RED AND ME... HAS TO FIGHT YOU!
PING
GRANDFATHER... IF YOU'RE THE WINNER OF THE FIRST MATCH... THAT MEANS...
FAN FAN
I'M BOWING OUT. YOU TWO ARE ON YOUR OWN...IN THE FINALS!
!!
...THE FINAL MATCH!
...THE SCHEDULED SECOND SEMIFINAL IS NOW...
!
SINCE TOURNAMENT RULES PROHIBIT THE LOSER OF A SEMIFINAL FROM CONTINUING...
WE HAVE JUST BEEN INFORMED THAT THE WINNER OF THE FIRST SEMIFINAL MATCH, DR. O, HAS WITHDRAWN FROM THE COMPETITION!
MURMUR... MURMUR...
DIDDLING
YOUR ATTENTION, PLEASE!

...TO DETERMINE THE CHAMPION OF THE INDIGO PLATEAU POKÉMON LEAGUE!!
HOOORAAAY
CONTESTANTS WILL ENTER THE ARENA...
TMM
TMM
SNAP
SNAP
Red vs. Blue
40
A Charizard... and a Champion
READY...
FINAL MATCH !!
I CAN'T STAND THE SUSPENSE! WHAT'RE THEY GONNA OPEN WITH?!
GULP
THEY'RE CHOOSIN' THEIR POKÉ BALLS...

WOK
WHEN THE POKÉ BALLS HIT THE GROUND...
HUSHHH
VNNN
FIGHT !!
BOM
BOM

VEEN
VENUSAUR !
CHARIZARD !
CHARR

DANG THE LUCK! DANG IT!!

GRASS VS. FIRE !!

FIRE SPIN !
...SOMETIMES YOU LOSE!
SAURRR
GRASS? I TAKE IT YOU WERE BETTING I'D LEAD WITH A WATER-TYPE POKÉMON. WELL, RED, WHEN YOU BET...
HEH

YOU WON'T SLIP OUT OF THIS!
GAH!!
CHAR
MINE !!
SSS
BOOF
?!
CAREFUL, BLUE! DON'T GET COCKY!
POISON... POWDER ?!
WOBBLE !!

SHH
SHH
SHH
NOW, WHILE IT'S WOBBLY– VENUSAUR, RAZOR LEAF!!
DON'T LET YER GUARD DOWN, RED!
SHNN
SHNN
HAH !
VIZZ
NO WAY!! GOOOOO...
SNORR
MEGA PUN–
BOM
...SNORLAX !!

SSS
BOM
SHMM
OH NO, YOU DON'T!
GRRNG
WHAT–?!
RRNG
SSSS
WHAT THE–?! FOUR ARMS?!
ROAR
LEGS ARE FREE!! MEGA KICK!!
HEH

HA
HAMP
GRIIIGRIII
GRIII
HO HO HO...
I CAIN'T TAKE MUCH MORE O' THIS...
LET'S SKIP THE CHEAP TRICKS, SHALL WE? SEE IF YOU CAN TAKE ME...HEAD-ON!
...

GRR
GRR
GRNG
NNN NNG
HAS THIS CHAMPIONSHIP EVER SEEN A WRESTLING MATCH LIKE THIS?!
HEH!
THIS IS S'POSED T'BE SNORLAX'S GREATEST STRENGTH— AND IT'S GETTIN' BEAT!!
OH NO!

I-IT'S LIFTING... THAT HUGE...
GRRRIIII
MA CHA MMMP
SHNORRRR
SNOR-LAX!
MACHAMP'S FOUR ARMS CAN BLOCK ITS OPPONENT'S PUNCHES AND KICKS SIMUL-TANEOUSLY!
NO USE STRUG-GLING.

WHOA...
ADD A LITTLE ROTATION...
VNNN
NOW...
WRRRN
WRRRN
...AND YOU'RE HELPLESS!
DA-KOOOOM
ACK!
SLAM!
A FOOLPROOF PLAN... AMAZIN' POWER... HAS RED GOT A CHANCE IN HECK?!

KRIK
KRIK
KRIK
TINKLE
KRAK
!!
TINKLE
IT BROKE THE ARENA FLOOR...
RRGH...
SSHHHHH
HEH
IF I RECALL CORRECTLY, RED, MACHAMP EVOLVED UNDER YOUR CARE... I'M GLAD TO HAVE THIS OPPORTUNITY TO SHOW MY APPRECIATION!

...
DON'T LET IT END, RED! C'MON NOW...
WELLLLL... I SUPPOSE IT'S TIME FOR THE FINAL BLOW...
THAT BOY'S THOUGHT O' SOME-THIN'!
HEH... I KNOW THAT LOOK O' HIS...
...
PLIIIK
YEAH! HE'S GOT SNORLAX USIN' HARDEN!
AN' PLAYIN' POSSUM FER THAT DUMB OL' BLUE!
PLIKK
!
MACHAMP! ATTACK!
MAAA

HIS FINAL MOVE !!
OHHH
HWOOOOOO
KARATE CHOP!
ATTA BOY! BLUE AIN'T CAUGHT ON YET!
THAT'S IT, SMARTY-PANTS...
WHEN THAT FIST HITS YORE ROCK-HARD SNORLAX...
...THERE'S GONNA BE ONE LESS ARM T' WORRY ABOUT!
PLIIIIIINK

!
...DO YOU HONESTLY THINK I DIDN'T ANTICIPATE...
NOW, RED...
VMMM
...YOU USING...
ZU. DOM MMM
...SUCH AN OBVIOUS TRICK?!
HM !
?!
!

NO!
FYOOOOW
SHHHH
BLUE READ HIM LIKE A BOOK! HE WARN'T AIMIN' AT SNORLAX... HE WAS AIMIN' AT THE FLOOR!
AS THE GREEK SAID, "GIVE ME A LONG ENOUGH LEVER..."
"...AND I CAN MOVE THE EARTH"!
FYOOOOOO

SAVE YOUR SLOGANS.
H-HEY... WAIT UP!
WHEN HE STARTED OUT, HE WAS TOO ARROGANT—TOO IMPRESSED WITH HIS OWN IDEAS. HE COULDN'T LET GO OF HIS PRECONCEIVED STRATEGY. HE'S LEARNED TO ADAPT TO SURPRISES.
SSH H
DESPITE HIMSELF, HE'S GETTING TO BE MORE LIKE...RED!
MY GRANDSON IS GROWING UP.
...
I'M NOT THE SAME TRAINER YOU BEAT BEFORE, MY FRIEND...
WHAT A BRILLIANT REVERSAL BY BLUE!
RED'S SNORLAX HAS BEEN FLUNG OUT OF THE ARENA!
ACCORDING TO THE RULES, ANY POKÉMON THAT TOUCHES THE GROUND OUTSIDE OF THE ARENA WILL BE INELIGIBLE TO...
Snorlax Out of Bounds

HWRRRRRR
?
HUH? WHAT'S TH-THAT NOISE?
!!
SPRKL
SNORRR
WAY TO GO !!
D-GOOOOM
DOUBLE-EDGE!!
THE SNORLAX! IT NEVER TOUCHED DOWN! IT'S HITTING FROM THE AIR!!
?!
EEEP

MAYBE YOU SHOULDA DONE YOUR HOMEWORK !!
I GUESS YOU DON'T KNOW HOW MANEUVERABLE A SNORLAX CAN BE, BLUE!

AND HOW TO SHORE UP HIS INSTINCTUAL APPROACH WITH HIS KNOWLEDGE... JUST LIKE BLUE!
RED'S LEARNING HOW TO KEEP HIS COOL...
MELT
TMP TMP
ARE YOU NUTS?! YOU'RE HEADIN' RIGHT BACK TOWARD THE ZOMBIES!
OO. THIS BLUE IS GOOD. NOT THAT I'LL EVER TELL HIM THAT...
THNK THNK
OOOWF
WAY TO GO, BULBASAUR! KEEP IT UP 'TIL YOU HEAR A GASTLY "BLORP"!
HMM... SO MY GRANDSON ISN'T THE ONLY ONE WHO IS GROWING UP!

BUT NOBODY WAS EXPECTING AN AERIAL ATTACK FROM YOU!!
PLAIN OLD KICKS AND PUNCHES COULDN'T BEAT THOSE FOUR ARMS—
GREAT JOB, SNORLAX !
MWIP

MA-CHAMP...

PAP
POM
!
KCH
YOU GAVE IT YOUR BEST. NOW RETURN TO YOUR POKÉ BALL.
I DON'T NEED TO LOOK AT MY POKÉDEX TO SEE WHAT CONDITION YOU'RE IN...
THERE WAS A TOXIC ATTACK IN THERE... YOUR HEALTH LEVEL'S DROPPED TO A THIRD...
SHHF
IS THIS THE SAME GUY WHO DIDN'T EVEN NOTICE WHEN A BABY KANGASKHAN WAS SICK...?
...
THERE'S AL BETTER NOW!
...
BOM
NOW... IT'S TIME TO FINISH THIS!
ALL RIGHT! LET'S SEE WHAT SNORLAX CAN DO AGAINST...
SNORRR
MAY-BE SO...
WHAT ARE YO DOING MY POKÉ E CAUGH IT?
NINETALES! THE ONE WE FOUGHT OVER BEFORE!

YOU'VE BEEN THROUGH ENOUGH, POOR GUY! YOU'RE NOT AT FULL POWER ANYMORE, ARE YOU?
OOPS! CANCEL THAT!
WOBBLE
FEH!
...IF YOUR OPPONENT'S AT A DISADVANTAGE.
COME ON. YOU KNOW IT ISN'T REALLY WINNING...
AND SOMEONE TOLD ME THERE'S NO SATISFACTION IN BEATING A WEAK OPPONENT. PICK YOUR NEXT POKÉMON, RED.
REMEMBER THAT.
HEY HEY HEY
KNOW YOUR LIMITATIONS. OR YOU'LL ONLY BEAT YOURSELF.
SOMEBODY TOLD ME ONCE THAT YOU'VE GOT TO KNOW YOUR LIMITS!
THESE BOYS HAVE LEARNED MORE THAN BATTLE STRATEGY FROM EACH OTHER.
HO HO!
AND THEY KNOW EACH OTHER LIKE THE BACK OF THEIR OWN HANDS!
HHHSSH
THEY'VE INCORPORATED THE BEST TRAITS OF THE OTHER INTO THEMSELVES...

RAAAAAAH
THIS MATCH IS AS TIGHT AS THEY COME! ONE MOVE COULD TIP THE BALANCE!

THE TIME IS NOW...
RTAK

COULD BE MY LAST CHANCE...
chik

BLUE'S GOIN' WITH NINETALES! WHAT D'YA ANSWER WITH, RED?!

HMM... ONE ELEGANT MOVE COULD WIN THIS THANG... AN' ONE DUMB LITTLE MISTAKE...
...COULD BLOW IT!!

FSH

BLUE!
RED!
RED!
WHO DO YOU LIKE BEST, BRUNO?
...
...
LOOK...
I SAY THE SULLEN ONE!
THE CHEERFUL ONE'S ABOUT TO MAKE HIS CHOICE...
HEH HEH HEH...

NIIIIN
WHAT'S HE WAITING FOR?!
NINETALES !
PLK
SHWIP
CHK
PF
PF
PF
FFFSS

FOOSH
WELL, IF YOU WON'T ATTACK...
PROBABLY GYARADOS OR...AERO-DACTYL !
SSS
HE KNOWS I'M GOING WITH A FLAME ATTACK. HE'S GOT FOUR POKÉMON LEFT! HE'S BOUND TO GO WITH A BIG ONE...
...I WILL !

DOES HE THINK A SMALL TARGET IS THE SAFER CHOICE?
THAT LITTLE THING ?!
POL
POLL
POLI-WRATH! ATTACK !
WRAAAAH!!
BOM
HWOOF
WELL, WITH THIS ATTACK, SIZE ISN'T THE ISSUE...
!!
FIRE BLAST !!
THIS NOT ONLY PREVENTS THE TRAINER HIMSELF FROM MOVING...

LOOSH
THE BLAST SENDS POLIWRATH'S WATER SPRAYING WILDLY–
...BUT FLINGS HIS POKÉMON UP IN A BLAST OF HEAT!!
HOOO

SSSSS
PIKA! POLI!
BLESH
POM
GOOD JOB, NINETALES! RETURN!
SHLRRRR
GNNG
CHAR-IZARD!
AND NOW, TO KEEP THE FLAME ATTACK GOING...
BOM
BLUE FOLLOWS FIRE WITH FIRE! HE'S GONE BACK TO HIS ORIGINAL POKÉMON!

BOM
VENUSAUR AGAIN?!
CHARR
WHAT NOW, RED?!
O... KAY...
IF YOU'RE GOING BACK TO CHARIZARD...
KCH
HMM...
YOU'VE GOTTA BE KIDDING.
IT'S AS IF RED IS MOCKING BLUE'S SECOND USE OF CHARIZARD! BUT HIS FIRST USE OF VENUSAUR WAS A DISASTER! WHAT IS HE THINKING?!
MRMR
MRMR

AND THIS TIME THE DANG FOOL DID IT ON PURPOSE!
HE'S SURROUNDED BY FIRE, AN' WHAT'S THE DUMMY DO?! HE THROWS GRASS AT IT?!
THAT IS SO VERY, VERY YOU...
HEH
YOU WANT US BOTH TO FINISH THE MATCH WITH THE POKÉMON MY GRANDFATHER ORIGINALLY GAVE US.
GWOOOO
AH. I GET IT, RED.
SAURRRR
CHARRRR
VENUSAUR!
CHOOSING SENTIMENT OVER VICTORY!
CHARIZARD!
SRRRRRRR
SRRRRRR

YOU KNOW THAT WON'T–
DO YOU ACTUALLY BELIEVE YOU CAN TIE UP A CHARIZARD?!
THAT'S NOT ANY OLD RAIN CLOUD...
RUMMMBLE
!!
HEY! WHAT'S THAT RAIN CLOUD DOING INSIDE?!
YOU DIDN'T THINK I WAS DUMB ENOUGH TO USE A VINE AGAINST A CHARIZARD, DID YOU?
HEH
THAT, BLUE, IS A THUNDER CLOUD!
AND WHEN THAT ENERGY BUILDS UP ENOUGH TO STRIKE...
PAXXX
PAXXX
...THAT'S BEEN CHARGED WITH LIGHTNING BY PIKACHU'S ELECTRIC ENERGY!
THE SUPER-HEATED WATER DROPLETS FROM POLIWRATH CONDENSED INTO A CLOUD...

RRRM
RRRM
KRA
IT'LL STRIKE THAT VINE !!
WE KNOW EACH OTHER !!
THESE THREE POKÉMON AND I HAVE BEEN THROUGH A LOT TOGETHER !!
CHARIZARD! BLAST IT AWAY!
IT'S A LIGHT-NING ROD!!

HE'S STILL BORN...
BUT WHO CARES!
IT HAS A BUD ON ITS BACK! COOL!
BULBASAUR
"BULB...A...SAUR."
BLISH
FSSH-H-
BULBASAUR IS A REAL MOUTHFUL.
YOU'LL NEVER OPEN THAT POKÉ BALL!
I'LL CALL YOU SAUR FOR SHORT.
GO, POLIWHIRL!
BOM
BLASH
YOU'RE MY BEST FRIENDS!
SINCE POLIWHIRL CHANGED...
BUT YOU DON'T...
...REALLY UNDER-STAND...
...FRIEND-SHIP!!
KRAK
B-LAMMMMMM

THAT'S... THAT'S...
THE FOG'S LIFTING!
?!
TOPPLE
AND THE WINNER IS...BL–
HSSSSSSS
CHARIZARD!
NO!
THE CHAMPION OF THE POKÉMON LEAGUE...
WOBBLE
GASSSP
!!
TOOOM

HOORAAAY!
...IS RED !!
WOBBLE
AFTER EVERYTHING WE'VE BEEN THROUGH TOGETHER... WE DID IT...
KWRRR
WE DID IT!
ROAR
ROAR
BWOT
...TO... GETH-ERRR...
PLEASE REMAIN SEATED FOR THE AWARD CEREMONY !
RED!
RED!

PiPiPi
HELLOOO? THIS IS GREEN! YOU KNOW...THE TRAINER WHO SNAGGED THIRD PLACE IN THE INDIGO PLATEAU POKÉMON LEAGUE! TEE-HEE...♡ NOW ABOUT THAT ENDORSEMENT DEAL...
HUH?
HEY, HEY! WHERE DO YOU GET OFF CALLIN' YERSELF—
SILLY BOY! PROFESSOR OAK WITHDREW, SO I'M IN THE RECORD BOOKS WITH THE THIRD BEST SCORE, AREN'T I?

SHE'S GOT US THERE!
GAK
HEH
COME ON! THEY CAN'T START WITHOUT YOU GUYS! HURRY UP!
WE HEAR YOU!
TCH! SHE'S SO OB-NOX-IOUS.

To be continued in the next volume...

POKÉMON

RED, GREEN & BLUE

Fin

COMING SOON IN VOLUME 4!
RAAA
IT'S BEEN TWO YEARS SINCE THE POKÉMON LEAGUE CHAMPIONSHIP BATTLE BETWEEN RED AND BLUE... NEW FRIENDS—AND NEW ENEMIES—AWAIT!!
A BRAND NEW ADVENTURE!!
VSH
POKÉMON ADVENTURES VOLUME 4!!
MEET NEW FRIENDS!!
JUMP INTO THE ADVENTURE!!

ADVENTURE ROUTE MAP 3

AFTER THE BATTLE OF SAFFRON CITY, RED MOVES ON TO THE CERULEAN CAVES. TRAVELING THROUGH THE VIRIDIAN FOREST, HE DEFEATS GIOVANNI, AND FINALLY ARRIVES AT INDIGO PLATEAU!

GOTTA CATCH EM ALL!!
ADVENTURE ROUTE MAP 3
FINAL SHOWDOWN WITH BLUE!
VS SPEAROW
VS CHARIZARD
INDIGO PLATEAU
CHAPTER 39
CHAPTER 40
VIRIDIAN CITY
CHAPTER 36
CHAPTER 37
CHAPTER 38
VIRIDIAN FOREST
REMATCH WITH GIOVANNI
VS DRATINI
GOLLLL
VS GOLEM
NIDO-QUEEN, ATTACK !!
VS NIDOQUEEN

RED'S POKEDEX!
ENCYCLOPEDIA
001 BULBASAUR
002 IVYSAUR
▶ 003 VENUSAUR
004 CHARMANDER
005 CHARMELEON
006 CHARIZARD
007 .....
008 WARTORTLE
009 BLASTOISE
010 CATERPIE
011 METAPOD
012 BUTTERF
TRAINER: RED
BADGES: 7
POKÉMON: 71
NUMBER CAUGHT
132
NUMBER FOUND
71
RED WON THE POKÉMON LEAGUE CHAMPIONSHIP, BUT HE STILL HAS A LOT OF POKÉMON LEFT TO CAPTURE...
RED'S TEAM AS OF CHAPTER 40
IVYSAUR FINALLY EVOLVED INTO VENUSAUR! THE CURRENT TEAM'S FINAL EVOLUTION IS COMPLETE!

POCKE

PIKACHU: L51
HP
NO.025

FURIOUS OVER THE ATTACK ON ITS VIRIDIAN FOREST HOME, PIKA WAILED ON GIOVANNI, THE LEADER OF TEAM ROCKET.

VENUSAUR: L60
HP
NO.003

IN THE DECISIVE BATTLE AGAINST TEAM ROCKET AT THEIR SAFFRON CITY SILPH CO. HEADQUARTERS, THE FLOWER ON SAUR'S BACK FINALLY BLOOMED!!

POLIWRATH: L61
HP
NO.062

POLI IS THE POKÉMON RED RELIES UPON MOST. WATCHING POLI RUSH HEADLONG INTO BATTLE IS A SIGHT TO BEHOLD!

SNORLAX: L52
HP
NO.143

DURING THE POKÉMON LEAGUE CHAMPIONSHIP AT INDIGO PLATEAU, LAX BATTLED BLUE'S MACHAMP. IT'S HARD TO BELIEVE THIS HUNGRY BEHEMOTH CAN GROW EVEN BIGGER—BUT HE CAN!

GYARADOS: L48
HP
NO.130

GYARA HAS A POWERFUL HYPER BEAM ATTACK! BUT JUST ONE LOOK AT GYARA IS ENOUGH TO MAKE AN ENEMY TURN TAIL AND RUN!

AERODACTYL: L41
HP
NO.142

AERO REALLY SHOWED ITS STUFF DURING AN INTENSE AERIAL BATTLE AGAINST MEWTWO! AERO AND RED FLY SO SMOOTHLY TOGETHER, THEY LOOK LIKE ONE CREATURE.

Message from
Hidenori Kusaka

Pokémon Adventures is already on its third volume! Now Red, Blue and Green charge into the Silph Co. headquarters of Team Rocket! What battles will unfold…?! Check out how everyone has improved!!

Message from
MATO

One battle after another!! I gripped my pen really hard while drawing this third volume. I felt like I was the one fighting as I drew the battle scenes… Take your time to enjoy this book. We finished every chapter just barely on schedule each month!

More Adventures Coming Soon...

Pokémon trainer Red goes off on a training challenge and... *never comes back!* But a tired and tattered Pikachu manages to return home by himself. A mysterious young trainer in yellow befriends Pikachu, and together they set out to find our missing hero!

And watch out for Team Rocket, Yellow Caballero... Could they be behind Red's mysterious disappearance?

AVAILABLE DECEMBER 2009!

What's Better Than Catching Pokémon? Becoming one!

Pokémon Mystery Dungeon

GINJI'S RESCUE TEAM

Ginji is a normal boy until the day he turns into a Torchic and joins Mudkip's Rescue Team. Now he must help any and all Pokémon in need...but will Ginji be able to rescue his human self?

Become part of the adventure—and mystery—with *Pokémon Mystery Dungeon: Ginji's Rescue Team.* Buy yours today!

www.pokemon.com

viz media www.viz.com vizkids

© 2006 Pokémon. © 1995-2006 Nintendo/Creatures Inc./GAME FREAK inc.
© 1993-2006 CHUNSOFT. TM & ® are trademarks of Nintendo.
© 2006 Makoto MIZOBUCHI/Shogakukan Inc.
Cover art subject to change.

Take a trip with Pokémon

ALL THAT PIKACHU!

ANI-MANGA™

Meet Pikachu and all-star Pokémon! Two complete Pikachu stories taken from the Pokémon movies—all in a full color manga.

Buy yours today!

Pokémon

www.pokemon.com

© 2007 Pokémon. © 1997-2007 Nintendo, Creatures, GAME FREAK, TV Tokyo, ShoPro, JR Kikaku.
© PIKACHU PROJECT 1998.
Pokémon properties are trademarks of Nintendo.
Cover art subject to change.

vizkids

viz media
www.viz.com

COWA!

WHO'S GOT THE CURE FOR THE MONSTER FLU?

From AKIRA TORIYAMA, creator of *Dragon Ball*, *Dr. Slump*, and *Sand Land*

MANGA SERIES ON SALE NOW

SHONEN JUMP
THE WORLD'S MOST POPULAR MANGA

On sale at **www.shonenjump.com**
Also available at your local bookstore and comic store.

COWA! © 1997 by BIRD STUDIO/SHUEISHA Inc.

RATED A FOR ALL AGES
ratings.viz.com

viz media
www.viz.com

JADEN YUKI WANTS TO BE THE BEST DUELIST EVER!

YU-GI-OH! GX

SJ

by Naoyuki Kageyama

MANGA SERIES ON SALE NOW

Only $7.99

SHONEN JUMP MANGA

Kazuki Takahashi
Naoyuki Kageyama

volume 1

SHONEN JUMP
THE WORLD'S MOST POPULAR MANGA

On sale at:
www.shonenjump.com
Also available at your local bookstore and comic store.

YU-GI-OH! GX © 2005 by Kazuki Takahashi, Naoyuki Kageyama/SHUEISHA Inc.
© KTakahashi
© NAS/TV TOKYO

RATED A TEN ALL AGES

viz media
www.viz.com

DINOSAUR HOUR!

Prehistoric Pranksters

A collection of comics featuring the goofiest bunch of dinosaurs ever assembled. Is the Jurassic period ready for their antics? Are you?

Find out in *Dinosaur Hour*— buy your manga today!

On sale at **store.viz.com**
Also available at your local bookstore or comic store.

vizkids
www.vizkids.com

www.viz.com

KYORYU NO JIKAN © Hitoshi Shioya / POPLAR Publishing Co., Ltd.

Backwards Game

BakéGyamon

A high-stakes game pitting monster against monster. Does Sanshiro have what it takes to win?

Find out in the *BakéGyamon* manga—buy yours today!

On sale at store.viz.com

Also available at your local bookstore or comic store.

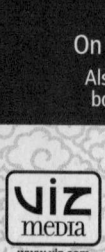

www.viz.com

www.vizkids.com

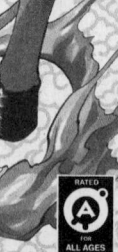

ratings.viz.com

BAKEGYAMON © Mitsuhisa TAMURA, Kazuhiro FUJITA/Shogakukan Inc.

D0035755

Pokémon®

DIAMOND AND PEARL ADVENTURE!

A BRAND NEW QUEST

Can a new trainer and his friends track down the legendary Pokémon Dialga before it's too late?

Find out in the *Pokémon Diamond and Pearl Adventure* manga—buy yours today!

On sale at store.viz.com
Also available at your local bookstore or comic store.

© 2008 Pokémon.
©1995-2008 Nintendo/Creatures Inc./GAME FREAK inc.
Pokémon properties are trademarks of Nintendo
Pokémon D•P Pocket Monster Diamond Pearl Monogatari © Shigekatsu IHARA/Shogakukan Inc.

vizkids
www.vizkids.com
RATED A ALL AGES ratings.viz.com
viz media
www.viz.com